Up in Smoke:

A New Friend and Foe

Written By: Amelia Lucas
Published By: Shawn M. Lucas
© 2023 Amelia Lucas
All rights reserved.

Amelia's Bookshelf Emporium
WHERE EVERY PAGE HOLDS A WORLD

Copyright Notice

Copyright © 2023 by Amelia Lucas

All rights reserved. No part of this book may be reproduced or transmitted in any form or by any means, electronic or mechanical, including photocopying, recording, or by any information storage and retrieval system, without written permission from the author, except for the inclusion of brief quotations in a review.

Published by Shawn M. Lucas

Cover Design: Annette Marie

Interior Design: Amelia Lucas

Disclaimer about any resemblance to real persons or events:

This is a work of fiction. Names, characters, places, and incidents are either products of the author's imagination or are used fictitiously. Any resemblance to actual events, locales, or persons, living or dead, is entirely coincidental.

Prologue

I remember when we first got back home, everyone suddenly knew our names. People were screaming and shouting at us, but not in a bad way. It was a celebratory yell. Everyone was happy about how we saved them. They saw us as their heroes and were in awe of us.

Blurs of flashing lights and questions were overwhelming me, and I had to dart inside. I leaned over the sink, splashed water on my face, and tried to calm down. Voices from outside were yelling constant questions that my brain had to quickly decipher: *Where did she go? What happened to the asteroid? What are the weird, new creatures that came here?*

Then there was a hand on the small of my back, a familiar touch I had come to love. When I turned around, her features were contorted in a worried expression.

"What's wrong, Natalie?" Sylvia asked me as she reached to grab my hand. Her voice and tone were soft, gentle, and reassuring.

"There's too many things happening, it's too overwhelming," I blurted out. She had gently placed her hand on my cheek as she looked into my eyes and said:

"I can calm the crowd for you if you don't want to talk about what happened. You don't have to do anything that you don't want to do. I can go out and speak to the media myself, if that's what you're most comfortable with. Whatever you need me to do."

I shook my head. "No, that's not what I want, I don't want to leave you alone. That is selfish." After I took a few deep breaths and told myself it would be okay, I looked at the bathroom door. I nod. "Okay, let's go." I paused once more and smiled. "However, I do like the 'calming the crowd' idea." She smiled and kissed me softly before nodding her head, agreeing with me.

We both walked out of the house and went outside. The waiting crowd roared with questions as we came into view. We stood on our porch to avoid being *in* the crowd. People continued screaming questions at us until Sylvia's voice broke out over everyone else's, "ONE AT A TIME, PLEASE!" she yelled. They seemed to calm down a bit after she had spoken.

Finally, someone came forward with a microphone in her hand and a camera poking out behind her back, she spoke hastily, "What happened with the asteroid? Did you direct it away from Earth?"

I reached down and grabbed the microphone from her since she extended it to me. "There never was an asteroid," I began. After I said that everyone became silent, waiting for me to continue. "Initially that was our thought, but we found out that it was an extra-terrestrial spaceship that had disguised itself as an asteroid."

Everyone around the reporter chatted amongst themselves and whispered another question into her ear. Someone handed her another microphone. "Why were the aliens here? Did they want to kill us?" Everyone began chatting again until Sylvia raised her hand, palm facing the crowd, trying to get the crowd's attention.

When everyone went silent, I looked at Sylvia, tilted my head, silently saying, "Do you want to take this one?" with my face. She took the microphone and gave me a small smile. "No." She began directing her attention back to the crowd. "They did not want to kill us. The ones that were violent and aggressive, were merely protecting themselves. We befriended one, his name is Erin. He told us why he was here." She pauses for dramatic effect, and I can't help but smile to myself as I thought about Erin. "It was to protect us. To protect Earth and our species."

"Protect us from what?!" Someone had yelled.

I cringed as I looked at her, not knowing if it was wise to talk about governmental affairs with the world.

"That is classified information." She said it so confidently, and I couldn't help but think that she had just read my mind.

"Did it have something to do with World Federal Space Agency? I saw fire and smoke coming from the building!" I remember being annoyed by how good some people's attention to detail is.

"Yes, it did." I said, wanting to supply some honesty for them, even if I didn't have to. That made the crowd roar with additional questions; their curiosity was peeked, and that may have been too much information to share with them. After that, everything was a blur. I remember police officers forcing the crowd to disperse and leave us alone. Sylvia handed the microphone back to the reporter and we went inside. I followed her blindly, not knowing or being aware of what was going on around me.

About three months after the interview, we decided to write a book about our experience with the Stellarborns (the species that descend from humans) and how we saved the planet. Sylvia and I worked day and night collaborating on the book. We started from the very beginning. Starting with how Darryll, my ex-co-worker, had brought the "asteroid" to my attention. Then how everything unfolded. How I had an epiphany and came to terms with it being aliens, and not actually an asteroid. How Sylvia saved me from dying, and then our journey to the World Federal Space Agency (WFSA).

As we worked on it, I learned how obsessed Sylvia could get over things like this. I never knew she was similar to me in this way. After a lot of long hours, we announced we'd be publishing a book about our adventures on social media. Thousands of people were excited and started blowing up our comment sections in all of our social media platforms! It was amazing and terrifying, all at the same time. Since we released the book, our lives have changed significantly. Neither of us can figure out if it is for the better or worse.

Before we published the book, we got permission from the proper agencies so we could expose the Government and WFSA's truth. Apparently, that was better for the companies and for the government, instead of suing them, we exposed their mistakes and blunders that led to the catastrophe. We could've sued for *a lot* of money, but instead we chose to take the high road. I guess trying to enslave a race is not the best thing to do, and we helped stop that from happening.

Once we came to an agreement with the government and WFSA, we released our story everywhere: paperback, hardcover, eBooks, and audiobooks. It hit all the big publishing companies within a few days! Our book sold out within the first week, and we had to mass produce more. We were stunned and excited, as we flew around the world, signing book copies, and talking about our experiences with Erin and our adventures.

The entire situation was overwhelming, and a year later, it is still a lot to wrap my head around. I quit my job to keep up with the publishing demands. Losing my job didn't matter very much, though. We made millions from our book. Plus, we came to a settlement agreement with WFSA for their part in trying to enslave humanity with the "Harmoney infusion". It was a secret settlement, but it basically stated to "not sue us." We were shocked that the founder of WFSA talked to us himself! He introduced himself as "Benjamin L. Anderson." It was all very surreal.

The most ironic part of it all was that we were *never* planning on suing. He didn't need to know that though. We just nodded and smiled our way through his whole speech. We made an agreement with him that in addition to the money, we could also request help at his facility whenever we needed it. He said, "If you ever need to put in a request for anything at any of our facilities, we will quickly get you whatever you need as soon as possible." His voice was quivering, as he told us this. I had to turn my head away so he couldn't see the grin creeping onto my features. It was amusing to see a multi-millionaire scared of some little nobodies like us.

Chapter One: A Fresh Start

Almost immediately after we brought WFSA to justice, Erin, the first Stellarborn we engaged with, went back to his time in the future. As a going away gift he introduced us to an intriguing device he called "The Chrono Nexus." It allows us to freely travel between his time and ours. Additionally, he guaranteed us that his device would enable instantaneous communication with him.

When he mentioned the device's name, we were both perplexed by what it meant. We asked him to explain the name's meaning, and he told us the word 'Chrono,' is rooted in the word 'time.' This illustrates the device's sole purpose, and 'Nexus' signifies its assignment to connect or link something or someone. Thus, this device's name signifies its time-traveling capabilities.

Knowing this we couldn't help but question, "Why can't you just *see* into *our* future?" It would be a reasonable assumption to think he could have such powers since he's from the future. He clarified that our timelines have been disconnected from each other and swiveled in two different directions. In his timeline, there was no point in which a different race traveled back in time to save another race. So, from that point the second his race went back in time, it changed the current timeline of Earth.

We watched as Erin pressed a button on The Chrono Nexus and stepped gracefully into the portal that opened. We haven't spoken to or seen Erin since that day.

I knew that being famous would not be easy. It seems like we're always looking over our shoulder when we're out in public, shopping, walking around the neighborhood, or just going out to eat. Everything we do is more challenging, but we try not to pay attention to people pointing at us or gawking at us. Sometimes it's challenging.

It is now a year later as I bolt down the front steps, and head down to the shoreline that my house overlooks. My sandals fill with sand as I take elongated steps onto the beach. I pause for a moment to take in a breath, savoring the scent of the salty air and the noise of the waves caressing the slopes of the beach. *Whoosh, whoosh, whoosh.* It's midday, the sun is high in the sky, not a single cloud to be seen. Perfect weather to take a dip in the ocean. My eyes catch a glance of a familiar figure sprawled out on a towel. I giggle and decide to give her a little scare. I creep closer, trying to be quiet, slowing my pace as I get close to her. She's wearing sunglasses so I can't tell if her eyes are closed or not. I assume they're closed by her slow breathing so she's probably pretty relaxed...not for long.

My heart beats quickly as I crouch down near her. "BOO!" I yell as I tap her shoulders to enhance the scare factor. Her whole-body jolts up, forcing her to sit upright. She takes her sunglasses off and looks at me. I have a goofy smile on my face, but she tries to stay serious even as I blurt out, "You should've seen the look on your face!" After the words spill out of my mouth I erupt with laughter, and tears roll down my cheeks as I belly laugh. I fall over onto my back, unable to compose myself, my mind replaying the scene in my head.

"Oh, my God Natalie!" She says, trying to make her voice louder than my obnoxious laughter. "I was so comfortable too!" She continues, annoyed but also a little bit jokingly. I attempt to sit up, but she gently and playfully pushes my shoulder as she rolls her eyes. "It wasn't even that funny!" She mutters.

"Yes!" I say, sitting up. "Your face was all." I widen my eyes, open my mouth, and gasp, recreating her expression. She pouts at me and crosses her arms. I can't help but maintain my smile.

"Awe, come on, it was pretty funny," I say, pouting back at her, mimicking her.

The corners of her lips begin to perk up into a smile. "Okay, yeah...it was a *little* funny." Sylvia says as a full smile breaks across her features.

I stand up and offer a smile back. "Come on, let's go swim!" I say as I strip my shirt and shorts off, revealing a white and black two-piece. The top boasts crisscrossed straps that elegantly support my breasts. The cloth wraps aesthetically around them to balance comfort and allure. The bikini bottoms slide up my hips, hugging them gently for a comfortable fit.

Her eyes widen when she sees me, her mouth slightly ajar. Her eyes trail up and down my body unforgivingly. "When did you buy *that?*" She says it so quietly that I can't help but tease her.

"Hm? Did you say something?" I ask as I extend my hand. She grabs it and I pull her up. She is still gawking at me, almost as if she never heard what I said.

"Oh!" she exclaims, finally deciphering my words. "Nothing." She adds quickly with a shy chuckle. She shakes her head and looks away from me as a blush grows on her cheeks.

"You're so cute when you're flustered." My tone is light and cheery. "Come on let's go swim!" I add getting ever so slightly impatient. I keep her hand held as we run down to the shoreline. She trails behind me, laughing and giggling.

I twitch when my body comes into contact with the cold ocean water. When I run deeper into the ocean, my legs give out underneath me and I tumble forward, losing my balance and taking Sylvia down with me in the process. We make a huge splash that causes us both to erupt with laughter. Still laughing we attempt to stand but I tumble back into the ocean again, water splashing into my face. An unpleasant taste of saltwater fills my mouth and I quickly spit it out in disgust.

"Geez! Do you need some swimming lessons, Natalie? You're not the most graceful swan in the bevy!" she puffs out in between laughing breaths. I grab her and I pull her down with me, to get her back for teasing me.

"You're such a bully!" I say to her when she sits up in the water.

"Right! Says the one who just pulled me into the water! How about the time you scared me, waking me up from my peaceful slumber, remember that?" She smiles at me as she continues to tease me.

I let out an exasperated gasp. "Oh please! You know you like it!" I say, pretending to be offended.

"So do you!" she says, biting her lower lip trying to hide the smirk playing on her lips.

I pout. "Don't look at me like that."

"Like what?" She looks around innocently.

I sigh. "Come here," I say as I extend my arms for her. She walks into my arms, and I wrap them around her. She rests her head on my shoulder and lets out a sigh of comfort. Her arms hold me, squeezing tightly. When I back away there's a cheeky grin on her face. "What?"

"Oh, nothing," she comments, dismissively, a smile still playing with her features. I narrow my eyes at her, confused.

"That's your catchphrase, isn't it. You really like those words." I say, more of a statement than a question.

She chuckles. "I suppose so, yes." She thinks for a moment then quickly grabs my hand and pulls me deeper into the water, now waist deep.

I dive under, fully submersing myself under the light blue, transparent liquid. I see her little legs swinging back and forth, keeping her body above the water. I burst up through the surface, and I begin to tread water as I look at her.

"Have you always liked to swim?" she inquires, thoughtfully. Her eyes locked onto mine.

I nod. "Yes." I pause for a moment to form more words. "Before my parents passed away, I always went swimming with my friends any chance I could get!" I say finally, a smile on my face.

"Why did you stop?" She swims a little closer as she listens intently.

"We moved." I look down sadly and chew on my lower lip. "When they died, I was put into the foster system then I was transferred from California to Chicago, Illinois. It was awful, really."

"Here." She swims to shore and sits down where the water meets the sand. I follow her and sit next to her. "Tell me about it."

My eyes search her features, studying her, before falling to my lap. "Living in California, we didn't really live in the cities. We lived in Davenport; its population now is around 600 people. It hasn't changed much, but I had a lot of friends there! Then my parents passed." I pause, taking a deep breath. Her hand finds mine and gives it a reassuring squeeze. I look at her briefly and I offer her a small smile before continuing. "I was put into a dilapidated house with 10-15 other foster kids. All the kids had awful backstories tied to them. Me? I was just a normal girl...I had a normal life, my parents had a steady income, and I didn't think anything bad was going to happen." I sigh. She rubs the back of my hand with her thumb. I scoot closer to her and rest my head on her shoulder.

I continue, "One day I was told a family was interested in me! I was elated! At the time I was around twelve, thirteen, or fourteen. I don't entirely remember. Soon after they adopted me, we flew to Illinois and settled into my new home. It was okay, 3 bedrooms, 1 bathroom. The location was just awful though. The crime rates were through the roof, and the amount of poverty was deadly."

"My foster family moved into that house because it was cheaper, and I was fortunate enough to actually have a good place to rest my head." I look up at her, my eyes boring into hers, waiting for a reply.

"I'm sorry, honey," she whispers. "I can't imagine how hard it must've been to leave the ones you loved, your friends." She pauses briefly before adding, "Did you not have any other family members though? Grandma, Grandpa? Aunts or uncles?"

I shake my head. "No. My family is small, the ones I did know were too old to take care of me, or simply didn't want to. I tried."

She runs her hand through my hair as I talk. Her eyes focused on my words and the experiences that she is learning about. She leans her head against my forehead. "I am proud of you. You're so strong, Natalie. All the shit you were put through as an adolescent, shines through to shape how you are now. You're such a smart little lady." I smile at her comment, I lean in, and kiss her gently. My hands cup her cheeks softly.

"Thank you," I whisper.

"You're very welcome." She looks down at her watch. "Hungry?" she asks, changing the topic. "It's time to start dinner."

"Yes! All that bullying from you really creates an appetite!" She scoffs and stands up, extending her hand.

"You're such a dork." She smiles, pulling me up. We walk to the towels, and I watch as she gathers them and our clothes. I link arms with her as we walk up to the house.

Chapter Two: Conflicted Ideas

"What are you fancying right now?" She calls out from the kitchen as I change out of my bathing suit.

"Do I have some options?" I ask as I stroll out of the bedroom and lean over the island in the middle of the kitchen.

"Yes! Whatever your little heart desires." She turns to face me and smiles and copies my posture.

I quirk and eyebrow up, a sly smirk playing with my lips. "Hmmm," I begin as I look her up and down. She tilts her head to the side, thoughtfully and narrows her eyes at me. "How about spaghetti with meatballs?" I say finally, standing up right.

"Sure! Coming right up." She replies in a cheery tone. I swivel around the counter, and I grab two pots for her, one for the noodles, one for the sauce. I grab out the ingredients needed from the cupboard, and I watch as she does her magic.

"I am going to go shower quick," I say to her. She turns to me and pecks my cheek, tenderly she lingers as she whispers in my ear.

"Alright, honey. No rush." I put my hand on her cheek, and kiss her softly, a smile written all over my features. My lips linger against hers, savoring the kiss before I walk away and into the bathroom.

"Mmm! It's delicious!" I praise as I take generous bites of the pasta.

"I'm glad you like it! I'd like to think I am a pretty good cook! Not to brag or anything." Sylvia jokes with a playful smile on her face.

As I was about to reply to her, the doorbell rings. I look at her perplexed. She shrugs her shoulders. I walk over to the door, wondering who it would be. When I open it, I come face-to-face with a familiar friend.

"Erin! What're you doing here?" Sylvia asks, beating me to the punch. I am startled, not knowing she was behind me. I turn around to look at her and she smiles at me which warms my heart.

I step to the side, and I gesture for him to come in. He offers a weary smile and obliges. He follows us to sit down on the couch, him in the middle. Sylvia and I watch as he fiddles with his sleeves and continues to look around nervously. I have a sneaking suspicion he's not here for a house party. "Erin?" I ask, finally, breaking the uncomfortable silence. "Is something the matter?" I quickly add.

He sighs and shakes his head and nods it all at once.

"It's okay, you can tell us. It's why you came isn't it?" Sylvia reassures.

"Something in the Stellarborns world...our world...has sparked some...issues that have caused our people to panic." He closes his eyes before he continues "I didn't know who else to ask besides you two." I scrunch my eyes as he speaks. Something about the way he is talking, so slowly and quietly like he thinks someone will hear him, makes me think it something very bad. I shoot Sylvia a sideways glance wanting to see how she's taking this information. She seems a little more relaxed than I am.

"Of course? What is it?" Sylvia asks him. After she speaks her eyes instinctively shoot to mine. She notices the worry spreading across my face and gives me the 'It's okay' look before returning her gaze to Erin. I wish Erin didn't sit in the middle so I could hold Sylvias hand.

He takes a few deep breaths before beginning. "A civilization we have come to befriend has announced an impending threat on their planet..." he trails off and shakes his head quickly. "We don't know how big this threat currently is, but it could develop into a catastrophic intergalactic cataclysm." I scrunch my eyebrows together, trying to figure out what that means. He looks from me to Sylvia as he continues. His words spill quickly out of his mouth. "AKA a war."

I tilt my head to the side and raise my eyebrows. "Our friends, the Astrans, have spotted deadly warships coming towards their home planet!" His voice begins to rise, but his angry tone is not directed at us. "We don't know who these creatures are, but the Astrans fear that their entire civilization is at risk of annihilation!" I watch as he grinds his teeth, making an awful screeching noise. Perhaps trying to hold back his anger. I scrunch my hands into fists, trying to keep myself from having a panic attack. I take a few deep breaths. Sylvia gives me a worried expression from across the couch.

He continues, "We've tried hard to mediate and negotiate with this race, but it seems as if these warmongers are hell-bent on annexation. We aren't sure what they want, or who they want. We desperately need more allies, like you humans, to help us! Perhaps your unique perspective and experience with dealing with past crises could be beneficial in preventing or winning this potential interstellar war." Help. He wants help. He wants *us* to go out of our way, travel through space and time, to a planet for people we don't even know to help stop a maybe unstoppable race?! "We're asking your species to go out of your way to travel dimensions to help us win something that may not be winnable, are you up for the challenge?" He looks at Sylvia and then at me. It's clear, at the moment, I am *not* ready for the challenge.

"Erin, please excuse us for a second. I think we need to talk this out." Sylvia stands up and for a moment I don't register it. I just keep rocking back and forth repeating his words in my head. *Help.* He wants help. He wants help. I feel a soft hand on my shoulder, which makes me look up. "Honey," her soft voice whispers. "Come on." She grabs my hand and gently pulls me off of the couch.

"Give us a moment, Erin," Sylvia remarks.

He nods. "Of course."

She yanks me into the bedroom and closes the door. She sits me down on the bed, but I quickly stand up and pace back and forth. My breath rapid as I say, "Help, help, help," repeatedly.

"Baby!" She says, interjecting my thoughts. She walks towards me and grabs my hand. "Look at me, Natalie! Keep your eyes on me, take a deep breath for me."

"I can't! I can't! I can't!" I cry out, tears stream down my cheeks.

"Don't think about Erin, sweetie. Just focus on me. Focus on us. Okay?" I nod my head quickly as I continue breathing rapidly. She wipes tears away from my face and says, "Deep breaths, honey. Breathe in...and out." I do as she says. I find her hand and I squeeze it, as I reach for her other hand and put it on my cheek. I take another deep breath, "Good girl. Now exhale, slowly." I let the air empty from my lungs, slowly as I keep eye contact with her. "You're doing so good, baby. Keep doing that, in and out." *Breathe in...and out...in...out.* I close my eyes and I rest my head on her forehead. "It's okay," She whispers. Tears are still streaming down my cheeks, but I am calmer now.

"This is too much," I mutter. Her arms wrap around me and squeeze me.

"Aww, sweetie." She whispers as she pulls away from me to wipe the tears away from my cheeks. "I promise you we can get through this, okay? You're strong, courageous, intelligent, and ambitious." I tilt my head down, but just as fast her hand is under my chin. "Beautiful." She finishes. I smile and nod stiffly. She leans into me and gives me a soft kiss. I let out a deep exhale as she does so. My muscles seem to relax as her lips press against mine. I rest my forehead against hers.

"Thank you," I murmur.

"You're welcome, Natalie." She rubs my back gently. Her hands run under the back of my shirt. She scratches my back which makes me melt in her arms. "Now, baby, what are your thoughts," she says cautiously.

I take a deep breath as I sit down on the bed and look up at her. "I don't know." I say finally.

She takes a seat next to me and gently rubs my back. "Erin is our friend. He helped us a year ago from becoming slaves to the government." She pauses to let what she said sink in. "I think we should help the Stellarborns and the Astrans. Even if we don't know the Astrans, we'd want them to help us if something like this was happening to us." I nod my head and I stand up.

"Let's go tell Erin." I say to her. She nods back.

We walk back into the living room, and I sit down next to Sylvia. This time Sylvia's in the middle. I am facing Erin.

"We had some time to discuss your dilemma," Sylvia begins. "We are willing to help you, Erin." His eyes light up as she says those words. "There's only one issue."

"Yes, yes, of course." He says quickly. "What is it?"

"You were a human once, so you know our society...we're not the most 'help anyone with everything' species," She asseverates. I cringe at her words, knowing she's right but also hating it.

He nods, thought-provokingly. "Oh yes. I know it too well. I am hoping people's empathy will shine through now."

"Okay, this all sounds great but how are we going to get...everything? Spaceships, manpower, firepower, etc?" I ask, logically.

"Natalie, do you remember when we had visited Benjamin?" she inquires. I scrunch my eyebrows together, trying to remember who that is.

"The founder of World federal Space Agency?" Erin interjects quirking his eyebrow up, but he doesn't have any eyebrows to quirk up, so it looks silly. "AKA me...?" He crosses his tentacles across his chest and looks at me annoyed.

"OHHH!" I say, finally remembering. "Right. What about him?" My genuine confusion is abundant and palpable. I feel a little clueless and I don't like that. Sylvia puts her hand on my thigh and smiles reassuringly.

"When we went to World Federal Space Agency, Benjamin said that if we ever needed something, all we had to do is ask. Remember? He was acting very nervous, looking everywhere except at us as he talked." I look at her, titling my head to the side. "All I am trying to say is, he could help us. Give us spaceships and resources to help. We could team up with the president as well. We know they're good friends. The president could supply guns, manpower, and the money that we need."

"Yes!" Erin exclaims. "That's a wonderful idea!" He nods hastily.

"They *do* owe us." I begin finally remembering what happened when we went to see him. "We saved the entire world from the Harmony Infusion, and we basically let their names slide. We could have named them as being part of the reason we were almost enslaved, but we kept their names out of it."

She nods with a smile. "Yes, Tomorrow morning, we can fly down to D.C. and talk to Benjamin about this. Perhaps ask for those spaceships and ask to talk to the president for allies and support."

"Ahh! This is why I came to you two! You all are so perceptive." He exclaims. He stands up and continues, "If you guys come across some new information, give me a call on your Chrono Nexus."

"Deal." Sylvia extends her hand, and Erin accepts, waving his tentacle up and down.

When he exits through the portal created by his Chrono Nexus, Sylvia looks at me and whispers in my ear, "I am never going to get used to the whole...tentacle thing."

I audibly laugh at her, and I lean in and whisper, "Me too. At least not for a while." She smiles and kisses me softly.

I look over to the dining table, our food still sits on the table. I walk over to it, and clean up the unfinished food, putting away the leftovers, while Sylvia slips into the shower. Once I finish, I strip down to a bra and underwear. Then I slide into bed. After a few moments, the shower turns off and her body fills the empty space next to me. A smile creeps onto my face. I get closer to her, and I run my hand down her arm.

"I am so glad you moved in with me," I whisper in the darkness. She closes the gap between us and wraps the blankets tighter around us. My leg slides on top of hers, as her arms wraparound my body.

"Me too, honey," She murmurs. She's so close I can feel her soft exhales against my lips.

I bite my lip before leaning in ever-so-slightly to kiss her lips. Her hand finds its way to my cheek, and she kisses me back. She brushes strands of hair behind my ear and kisses me again. "Goodnight," I whisper to her as I nuzzle my head into the crook of her neck.

"Goodnight, sweetheart." Her words are the last thing I hear before I fall into a deep and comfortable sleep.

The sun begins to peak out in between the window blinds, forcing my eyes ajar. I stretch my legs, as a low, satisfied groan escapes from my lips. When my eyes adjust to the lighting, I notice the absence of Sylvia. I look around the room for her, sit up and spot her sitting in the corner of the room, sipping a cup of coffee. I squint my eyes and shoot my eyebrows toward the ceiling.

"Good morning, sweetie." She stands up and sits down next to me, setting her coffee on the end table.

"How long have you been watching me?" I ask, confused, rubbing my eyes.

She thinks for a moment, "Not long." She brushes hair away from my face and smiles. "You're just so peaceful when you're sleeping." Her tone is equanimous and soothing. I squint my eyes since I am still encompassed with the after effect of sleep. I am barely able to make out her features, but I know she is smiling.

I flip out from under the blankets, and I crawl closer to her. I put my hand on her cheek and kiss her lips. Her body jolts, slightly, surprised by the sudden interaction between us. Soon the confusion is replaced with a soft sigh. She turns toward me, to get a better angle. Before I part, my lower lip captures hers, pulling it with my teeth, before letting it go. I lean in again, but she pulls her head away from me with a small smile on her lips.

"You should go clean up. I made coffee for the road," she says, reluctantly. I know she doesn't want to leave, and neither do I. I want to stay here, at this moment.

I nod. "Okay." She pecks my lips briefly before getting up and grabbing her coffee. I follow her out of the room, slipping into the bathroom to freshen up.

"So, have you come up with an extravagant plan?" I ask Sylvia, as she drives us to the airport.

"Well, Lucky for us, I called the airport this morning and they're willing to lend us one of their aircrafts. It took a little persuading but since we saved the world once, perhaps they think we will again." She shrugs. "That'll save us some money and time but besides that, not really." She sneaks a glance at me. "Do you?"

I giggle. "Not exactly..." I start. "Benjamin told us that he will help us no matter what. He owes us for trying to enslave our race and basically turn us into mindless zombies. I say we just march in there and demand that he helps us. He has no right to say no to us after what he tried to do."

Sylvia makes an amused chuckle. "And if they say no?"

"Then I remind him that we made a deal, if he breaks his part, we can break ours." If he wants to play mean, we can sue him. I know we'd win and so does he. That's why he paid us off because he didn't want us to sue him.

She looks at me biting her lip. "You're so attractive when you're being a boss woman." I look down at my hands.

I smile. "Thank you." I tuck a strand of hair behind my ear, suddenly feeling a little nervous. "I do my best." I think for a moment. "Hey, I have a question."

"Shoot."

"Why do you think Erin changed his name? If he is the creator of WFSA, then he is Benjamin in our timeline, right?" Of course, I already knew that I am just curious as to what made him want to change his name.

"Hm. That'd be a good question to ask him. Perhaps, so he didn't live in constant sorrow about what he did? A new beginning? Plus, Erin is a much easier-to-pronounce name!"

I laugh at her last remark. "All good points. Especially the last one!"

She smiles at me. After another hour or so of driving she finally says, "We're here."

We exit the car and head down to the plane they let us borrow. When we slip into the cockpit, I look at her and state, "I am getting hella Deja vu."

She chuckles. "Let's hope this is the *easy* part. Last time we almost got ravaged by a fricking dog!"

I chuckle at her. "Do not give me PTSD! That was very traumatic." I retort, playfully.

"Of course, of course," she replies as she sets the plane up. "How could I forget?"

Once we're in the air, I pull out my phone and dial Benjamins number. *Ring. Ring. Ring.*

"Hello, thank you for calling World Federal Space Agency. This is Natasha speaking. How can I help you today?" a feminine voice asks. Assumingly his secretary.

"Hello, this is Natalie. I was wondering if I could set up an appointment to speak to Benjamin." I say to the woman.

"Benjamin doesn't usually make appointments with people. May I have a last name?" she inquires.

"Harlow. Sylvia Palmer will be joining us." Silence lingers between me and the woman on the other end.

Finally, her voice breaks through the silence. "Of course. When you get here just check in with the front desk. They will direct you to his room. Thank you for calling." Before I can reply the phone hangs up. I look at Sylvia who looks amused by the call.

"Well then. They sound excited to hear from us," she says with a small chuckle.

"Mhm. I don't think anyone in the government will *ever* be excited to hear from us ever again." She nods.

"Yes, ma'am."

"Sylvia," I say after a while of comfortable silence. My eyes have been following the tops of the clouds, remembering the first time we were up here together. It doesn't seem that long ago.

"Yes, honey?" she asks me.

"Do you remember when you told me about your grandma dying?" I revert my attention towards her, reading her expression.

"Yes, I do," she says, crestfallen. Her eyes are somber. She's probably remembering what happened. I feel a little bad to ask because it clearly upsets her...I just want to know what happened.

"What happened? How did she die?" I ask her in a soft tone. Not wanting to offend her.

She takes a sip of her coffee before speaking. "Cancer." Her eyes dart to mine. "We were both in such denial about it...I thought that maybe she was just getting old, you know? She was slipping into her early 80s and that's when it *really* started to show. There'd be days when she didn't get out of bed...she wouldn't eat. Sometimes she couldn't eat. One day I finally took her to the hospital. I was fifteen. That day, I was told to leave her at the hospital so they could run tests. I had stayed at the hospital with her, hoping that maybe she'd get better, but that's when I found out that she was in the early stages of stage four cancer." She huffs out a deep breath. When I look at her, tears are streaming down her beautiful face. I reach for her hand, allowing her to feel her emotions. I doubt she's ever talked to anyone about this.

She continues her voice shaky, "I was heartbroken..." She shakes her head and breathes out noisily through her nose. "Even that's an understatement." She looks at me briefly before saying numbly, "They gave her five months. They said they could try chemotherapy and see if it helps, but they didn't think it was likely she'd make it. At this point, the cancer had spread to some vital organs and was rapidly growing."

I turn my body to face her, and I swipe tears away from her cheeks. She rubs her cheek against my hand, closing her eyes. Before she continues, she flips the plane into autopilot. "She made it longer than they thought...on my birthday, my sixteenth birthday, she passed. It's almost as if she was waiting to see the day." A small smile creeps on her lips, and I trace it with my thumb. She leans her forehead against mine. "I visited her every single day after school. I basically lived at that hospital for six months. She couldn't do anything for those months...her body was too frail. I am still amazed she made it as long as she did."

Chapter Three: An Unfortunate Meeting

The plane makes a swift landing on the runway. Luckily, the airport was expecting us, so nobody was thrown off by our arrival. We park the plane in the designated spot they gave us, and we climb into a cab waiting for us. Apparently, we're now considered 'VIPS.' I suppose it's because the last time we came here it wasn't exactly because of something cheery.

We climb into the cab and tell the person where we want to go. He gets us there quickly, and before we know it, we're walking up the very steps that I never thought we'd come back to.

"More Deja vu," I say to Sylvia with a sigh.

She chuckles. "Don't worry. It'll get worse!"

She opens the large entrance door to the WFSA facility, and I instantly know that she was right. The flashbacks start to fill my mind. The sound of Erin's voice yelling over the incessant sound of guns being fired and people crying out in pain. Images of the fire spreading out through the building and the two of us running away from danger intrude my mind. I reach for Sylvia's hand. My fear begins to take over before Sylvia squeezes my hand. I look at her. "Stick by my side, okay?" she whispers to me. "It'll be alright. I know it's hard to be back here."

I nod. We walk to this front desk that I didn't notice the last time we were here.

"Welcome!" A cheerful voice greets us from behind the desk. "I'll be with you in just a moment."

I rest my head on Sylvia's shoulder, ignoring the judgmental looks from others regarding our PDA. "No problem!" Sylvia returns in a cheerful tone.

"So, how can I-" The lady cuts herself off when she sees who we are. I look at Sylvia, her eyes are already on me. I give her a worried expression, and she squeezes my hand, reassuringly.

"Hello! We're looking for Benjamin."

"Why, yes of course! What is your last name?" The hurriedness in her voice and fast typing are not details I am going to let slide out of my mind. It is locked in my memories for now. *They fear us.*

"Palmer," Sylvia says, with confidence. I can't help smirk at her words. Confidence is not something that she lacks and that is attractive.

The lady's face droops downward, her eyes wide. I guess they weren't expecting us to actually show up. I don't know why she asked our last names because it was clear she knew who we were. Perhaps she wanted to make sure. "Yes, yes of course. We were expecting you two. Please, follow me."

We follow as the receptionist's feet swiftly move across the floor, and through the corridor. We pass the area that used to hold all the soon-to-be Stellarborns. They had to rebuild a lot of this building because it had been seriously burned during the battle. Glass shards are sprawled over the ground and bits of computer parts and miscellaneous technological parts are scattered about.

The clear, goopy liquid still sticks to the floor, making it shimmer in the light. *Interesting.* Perhaps they have been too busy dealing with the media and trying to get their story right. Or maybe they can't touch it because people don't want them to think they're going to use those parts again...

She opens a metallic-looking door, exposing what I assume is Benjamin's office. "He'll be right with you, please, make yourselves comfortable."

She closes the door behind us, allowing us to explore the room. Directly opposite the door is a wooden desk, a laptop sits atop it, and a leather chair behind it. Behind all of this is a large floor-to-ceiling window that spans the back of the office. Off to the side, sits a couple of sofas with a coffee table in-between. I glance at Sylvia and walk over to the window.

The office overlooks the garden in the middle of the facility. Along the edges, are blooming flowers of all kinds, roses, daffodils, and lilacs. Different colors paint the greenery of the spherical garden. I wonder how you'd get down there. It looks so peaceful and calming.

Mid-thought the door opens and a male presence is in the room with us. I look to find Sylvia, who is sitting on one of the chairs. I plop down into the chair next to her. She extends her hand out to me, and I take it.

"So." Benjamin begins as he sits down in his leather chair. He rolls his sleeves up, his eyes darting between us. "What can I do for you?"

I put my other hand to my chest, feeling my heart *bam, bam, bam* against my chest. I look at Sylvia, and she just smirks, knowing what I want her to do.

"We're here on behalf of a...friend." Sylvia seems so calm when she speaks, *I don't feel calm at all*. I chew on the side of my cheek, the room already feeling pretty tense.

"Proceed," He exclaims; and I take a deep breath. If he is nervous, he is not showing it at all.

"A friend of ours, his name is Erin, he's a part of the Stellarborn Species that we helped last year." Benjamin raises an eyebrow.

"Mhm, what about him?" I squeeze Sylvia's hand as she continues.

"He came to our house yesterday and told us some scary news." Her voice is calm, steady, unwavering. She crosses her arms over her chest and leans back in her chair, maintaining eye-contact with him. "His ally, the Astrans, have come into contact with a deadly force. It seems as if they're going to invade their planet and try to take them out with force." She makes a fist when she says force. "It sounds like the invaders are a new race that has yet to be discovered."

He stands up and rolls his eyes. I watch as Sylvia stands up as well, I stay seated. "And why do I care about this?" He asks his tone seeming annoyed and uninterested.

She rolls her eyes and shakes her head in annoyance. "Well. If you didn't help, there is a chance that we wouldn't have a race anymore." She says it like it's the most obvious thing in the world. "The Stellarborns are from the future. Their technology is way ahead of ours and if they can travel into the past, I am sure others can or they could easily figure it out. The Astrans are a more developed civilization, that has been around longer than us *and* the Stellarborns. Who knows what power they possess. Perhaps their attackers are even more powerful."

He scoffs. "I am still not following on why you need me. There are so many other people you could talk to, why me?" He looks from me to Sylvia. I can tell he's nervous now. His emotions are raw and palpable as he speaks. The tension in the room is growing and it is making me want to run away. I can't though, I must be strong for Sylvia.

"You have what we want. Rocketship's and a connection to others via your fame. You have the ability to do what you want with the resources you have and the people you know. That is what we need. Power, the ability to travel outside of our planet, and companionship. You can provide all of those things."

Before she continues, he cuts her off. "Please! Why would I bend over backwards for you and let you take my Rocketship's and let you use me for my power?" He jabs his finger at her and then hastily walks over to his door and opens it. "I think it's best you leave. I am not going to take this from you."

She walks over and slams the door closed. His eyes widen and he looks away from her. All bark no bite. "The last time we talked, the only time in fact, I remember you mentioning something along the lines of 'we *owe* you one for not suing us.' We saved your asses, and you know it! We brushed all the shit you did under the rug and did not call you out in our book per our agreement. So don't play victim here! Now sit back down and stop acting like a child!"

I watch as he slowly walks back to his chair and plops into it. He doesn't dare make eye-contact with us now, a significant change from before. "We want your rockets because we need to get to the Astrans planet. Our rockets are advanced enough to do that. We also need your connection to the president. He will help us gather all of the allies and resources that we need. Then the last, and most important step is to travel to Erin's time and help the Astrans." She is calmer now. She sashays back to her seat and sits. She crosses her legs.

"And what if I don't oblige?" he asks, finally looking up at us. I know he's bluffing by the way he says it. He tries to put confidence in his words, but it just turns into him feeling sorry for himself.

She chuckles. "Then we're going to sue you for everything you have. Not only that, but if you don't help us, everyone will hate you. They will spit upon your name. We censored a lot of what happened last year from the media, but the amount of damage we could do to you would ruin your reputation forever." She scoffs and rolls her eyes. "First, you try enslave all humans, then you put our race in danger of annihilation by not helping stop these people, and you'd let another race dwindle away?" She pouts mockingly. "I bet the media would love to hear that."

He looks at us, a sorry look on his expression. "How sad...all your power, fame, success...GONE. I'll pull the rug right out from under your damn feet. The same rug we put all your baggage under." She stands and starts to mime it out. She mimics herself grabbing a rug and pulling it towards her. She puts her hand against her forehead, like you'd do to shield yourself from a bright light, and she watches as someone falls, looking down. "*Splat,*" she says finally looking back at him. "Squashed. Like a bug."

"Might I interject?" I ask looking at Sylvia.

She smiles at me, changing her entire demeanor. "Of course, honey."

"It's also in your best interest to help," I tell him.

He crosses his arms. "How so?"

"The invaders, like we said, may have the power to travel in time and destroy *our* civilization too. We don't know what this civilization is capable of. If we can stop them, it would benefit us as well."

He points between the two of us, nodding and stroking his imaginary beard. "Uh-huh. You two are good...very good." He stands, and Sylvia sits down next to me again. I watch as he paces about the room, hands behind his back, waying out his options. "Alright." He says finally. "I'll help you." He nods again and looks at us. "What's your plan."

I look at Sylvia surprised, and she smirks. She knew she'd persuade him. She had the upper hand. *So attractive.* "We need help from the entire world really. You have a strong relationship with the Government, you must still have a few strings to pull, yes? And, again, you have the spaceships we need."

"Again...you're good." He puckers his lips before he sits back down in his seat and drapes his leg over the other. "Yeah, I do."

"We want a meeting with the president, Sebastian Montgomery, and *you* are going to come with us."

"And why do you want me?" Benjamin asks.

"You had teamed up with Sebastian already and you aren't the one who blew up all their *important* equipment. We are. If you're there he may find it a necessity to help. You're an important piece to a very complex puzzle. For us you serve as transportation and for them you serve as, not only a friend, but of someone of high importance that the government trusts and respects. You're our key."

He nods and stands. Reluctantly he says, "Well, let's go. I will book an appointment with him. Since we're friends, he's more likely to let us in at will." I raise my eyebrows thinking, 'yep, that's why we need you.'

"I can find a limo for us," He adds. "The White House is in D.C., and it isn't a long drive. Maybe 13 minutes." I watch as he pulls out his phone and appears to send a brief text, before looking back up. "Okay, I texted Sebastian. He said he's in a meeting currently but will be out by the time we get there."

"Alright," Sylvia says, as she stands up. I join her and we walk out of the office and into a winding corridor. I hold her hand the entire way out. When we exit the building, a black limo is waiting for us.

Chapter Four: A Trip to the White House

"Is that for us?" I ask Sylvia, wide-eyed.

"Welcome to luxury, Mlady." She bows and kisses my hand. I giggle and get into the limo. I gasp when we step in. I am blown away by a white leathery interior. A long couch extends against the far wall and curves around the corners, into a U shaped-sectional sofa. The floor is a rich shade of brown, almost like a cup of coffee. It contrasts nicely with the white of the couch, walls, and strip of gold that runs through the center of the roof in a wavelike pattern. In front of the seating area is a bar that is built into the wall. This bar has a variety of alcoholic and non-alcoholic beverages. All different kinds of beverages are available, anything from fine wines to different kinds of brandy. Cylindrical diamond glasses sit in rows waiting to be filled.

Behind the alcohol, a glowing golden light shimmers and shines illuminating the bottles with a bright color.

"Jesus, this must've cost a fortune!" I gasp.

Benjamin chuckles, almost sounding amused. "Well, perks of being famous. It didn't cost me a dime. It comes with fame and having a fortune!" After he said that I am taken back to the first-time meeting Erin and how he said, "Because I am the one who unleashes the elixir." *I can't believe two people can be the exact same, but so different.* Erin is kind, generous, and thoughtful. Whereas Benjamin seems to be kind of arrogant and off putting.

I raise my eyebrows, but I try to ignore his statement. I sit down and Sylvia sits next to me. "So comfy. Are you seeing what I am seeing, Sylvia? This is astonishing." I look around more as I wiggle in the seat, surprised by how comfortable it is.

She smiles at me and boops my nose. "You're so adorable."

Benjamin cringes and says, "Look...not to be a Debby Downer...but could you lower the PDA?" Benjamin asks. "It's just...I am not much of a fan."

Sylvia smirks. *Oh gosh. What is she going to say?* "Oh, trust me. This is nothing." She looks at me, raising her eyebrows.

I shake my head and I punch her shoulder. "Sylvia! That is inappropriate." I say the last part with a whisper.

"Hm? You didn't think that when-" I cut her off by clearing my throat.

"Okay! That is quite enough." I give her a dirty look and she just shrugs. I roll my eyes and sigh. "Anyways, Benjamin!"

"Hm?" he asks, reverting his attention to us.

"I'm curious about how you think this will all play out."

"Well, Sebastian Montgomery is a lenient guy, which is ironic since he's the president. I don't think it'll take much convincing for him to join us." He thinks for a moment.

"What makes you think that?" Sylvia budges in.

He puckers his lips again; I am beginning to think it's his signature 'thinking face.' He begins, "I've worked with him ever since he came into office, about two and a half years ago. He is a sucker for adventure and anything to give him more fame and political influence."

"Okay, but he probably isn't going to be very happy when two people come into his humble abode and try to force this on him," I say to him.

"Yeah, well. You did the same thing to me, and I caved. I am just saying, he will probably give in to you quicker. Plus, you have the upper hand. He's under the same obligation to help that I am. He helped me with my...goal...a year ago." I nod and Sylvia does as well. What he says makes sense and it makes me question why he acted the way he did previously.

Shifting the conversation I ask, "How did the driver know where to go?"

A sly smirk imprints on his features. "I texted him the coordinates ahead of time."

I nod. "Ah."

Just as it was going to get awkward the driver calls back to us, "We're here."

We get dropped off directly at the front entrance of the White House. We step out of the limousine, and my eyes must adjust to the brightness. When I can finally look at the building, I am awestruck.

This is a beautifully constructed building. The entrance has three stairwells, two of which give direct access to the second floor. There's a red rug leading into the front grand door of this building. There is a large, white, concrete deck with six pillars wrapping around the entryway. Above this is another large presidential-looking balcony. We head into the building, and a chaperone instantly greets us. He guides us through the beautifully decorated rooms. The walls are layered in marble that wrap around the rooms. The same can be said for the floor, which are stunning, darker tones of marble for some contrast. The ceiling appears to be made from wallpaper, with intricate designs imbedded into it. I hold Sylvia's hand as we walk out onto the porch opposite from where we came in. The chaperone guides us to West Wing and into 'The Oval Office.'

When we enter, the chaperone stands outside the entrance. I stand awestruck by the interior decor. There are two sofas in the center with a rectangular coffee table in the middle. On top sits a bowl of apples. The wallpaper is yellow, with stripes that are a darker shade of yellow. The floor is a contrast of brown, and a zig-zagged wooden pattern. Opposite the couches there is a fancy-looking wooden desk, with a dark brown wooden chair behind it. Beside that is a table, with a lot of picture frames on it. I assume family and friends of the president. Littered around the walls of the room are standing cupboards and chairs, along with old paintings and photographs.

I look over at Sylvia and she gives me a reassuring look and mouths 'You got this.'

"He usually takes his time to get here," Benjamin says. "We might as well seat ourselves."

"I'll sit in the middle," I say as I rush over to the couch and plop down in the center. Sylvia and Benjamin join me on either side. I lay my head on her shoulder, and I close my eyes.

"How did you two meet?" Benjamin asks reluctantly after cringing at us, but he is trying to fill the silence. I look up at Sylvia.

"I got this one!" I say, happy that I can finally answer a question. "I had gotten into an argument with a co-worker and was depressed. I dazedly went outside, and she saved me from getting hit by a car. This was at the beginning of the Stellarborns arriving on Earth."

"I see. That is quite the meet cute!" He says sarcastically but I don't catch it.

I chuckle. "Yes! It is. Meeting someone usually happens when you least expect it."

"Welcome back, Benjamin," a cheerful voice exclaims, cutting into our conversation. Benjamin stands up and shakes Sebastian's hand.

"I'm pleased to make your acquaintance again!"

"Mm, yes. It has been a while. Please, take a seat!"

He sits back down on the couch, while Sebastian sits across from us on his couch. "So, what can I do for you two?" He asks. Apparently, nobody gave him a heads up on what we were doing here. Maybe he doesn't remember us either. I don't think we met him anyway.

"Well, Mr. Montgomery..." Sylvia begins but he cuts her off.

"Please, that isn't necessary. Sebastian is fine!" Okay, he *definitely* doesn't remember us.

She raises a brow and lets it fall back down before she continues. "Okay...well, Sebastian, we got some news from a friend that the Stellarborn's ally, the Astrans, are in grave danger. A bloodthirsty extra-terrestrial species may try to annex them! Erin needs your help, your extraordinary political influence, to help fight for both the Stellarborns and Astrans."

He turns his head to Benjamin. Benjamin sighs. "Stellarborns are the race we were about to create! Remember? We were going to release the Harmony Infusion all over the world that would enslave our race."

"Ah, yes! Thank you, Benjamin. Now, who are these...Astans...what was it?"

"AstRans," Benjamin corrects. "They're allies with the Stellarborn species. They're being invaded by a different species."

This time, I butt in. "Mr. Mont-" I cut myself off "Sebastian," I begin with a sigh. "Look, I know this is a lot to ask but-" This time he cuts me off.

"Remind me. Who are you two? Do I know you?" he asks. His tone is changing, he sounds very defensive now.

"I am Sylvia Palmer, and this is Natalie Harlow. We were the ones to stop your plan over at WFSA."

He stands. "Okay, so you two expect me to help you when you ruined my plans? Is that what's happening here?" He walks away from us. Benjamin walks over to him and whispers into his ear. Sebastians face loosens into a smaller frown and then his eyebrows scrunch up. I wonder what Benjamin is telling him. Sebastian nods slowly. They both walk back to the couch and take their seats back. "What do you want from me? What if I don't help you?"

Sylvia sighs. She's sick of repeating herself, as am I. "You are in debt to us for not exposing that you were *trying to kill and enslave our race.*"

He nods. "So, you decide to stroll right into *my office* and *order me* to follow your plan without any sort of receipts or Documentation?"

Sylvia nods her head and speaks confidently, "Yes, that's exactly what we're doing."

He drapes his arm across the couch and puts his leg on top of his knee. He squints his eyes and rubs his chin with his fingers. "This is absolutely ridiculous." He looks at Benjamin. "But I do have to say. I love your enthusiasm and forwardness. No beating around the bush." He sighs. "Alright. I will help you."

"Really?!" I ask inquisitively and maybe a little too enthusiastically. I perk up in my seat.

"Yes, I suppose. What do we have to lose? Besides, you're right. I have to live up to my mistakes and maybe this'll help! I'm in debt to you and the entire world."

Benjamin stands up. "Yes, yes." He claps his hands together, a few times. "Chop, chop! We don't have all day to lounge around!"

"Benny! Take a chill pill! Relax." Sebastian takes a deep breath and points at him then at himself saying, 'Just breathe.'

"Urg." He groans. "No." He rolls his eyes. "Lives are at stake."

"I thought you didn't care?" Sylvia asks.

"You were talking about it so passionately like it means a lot to you and I have to admit, it is pretty admirable. Not everyone has the courage to walk into the president's office and demand that he helps them with something that could possibly be impossible. Sebastian get our troops together, we need a lot of them."

"Will do, Benny!" He looks at his watch. "You gals can sleep in a spare bedroom, the Lincoln Bedroom, your chaperone can show you the way."

"You're going to let us sleep in the white house?" I ask him.

"Yes. You're my guest and to be honest, I feel a little guilty for what I did and said to you two. It wasn't fair of me to be mad at you considering the things that I've done."

"Alright, thank you Sebastian." He nods. "When we wake up, we're going to go travel to the Stellarborn's timeline and meet up with Erin to see how we can help," Sylvia remarks as she stands up and looks over at me.

"Sounds good, here, I'll give you my secretary's number. She'll text you when everything is ready!" Sebastian hands us a notepad and pen, Sylvia writes down both of our numbers.

"Just shoot us a message when everything is ready to go. We will need to get another Chrono Nexus for you to travel with." Sylvia hands him his notepad and pen back.

He looks at us confused.

"I'll explain it all later. It'll make sense!" Sylvia says to him.

Benjamin exits the room and soon after Sebastian does as well. I turn to Sylvia, and I exhale a deep breath, "I know, baby," she whispers as she runs her hand along my cheek. "Let's go to the room. Get some shut eye. We have a long day ahead of us."

When we exit the Oval Office, I am surprised by how dark it is already getting outside. We follow our chaperone to our bedroom. The sun is setting below the horizon, looking like a painting splattered across the sky, with beautiful colors such as pinks, purples, blues, and tints of yellow. I wrap my arm around Sylvia's and rest my head against her shoulder. "So beautiful," I say. "It's breathtaking."

She turns and smiles at me. "That's something I've always admired about you."

"What's that?" I tilt my head to the side.

She looks me up and down, her hands caressing my arms. "You find beauty in things most people overlook. Yes, the sunset is beautiful, but most people see it so much they don't care. You aren't like that..." She pauses and chews her lip, looking down at our feet. "It makes me fall for you even more."

I open my mouth to say something, but nothing comes out. Instead, I lean up and kiss her soft lips. My arms, slink around her waist as I let out a deep breath, "Do you remember that first moment we kissed?"

"How could I forget?" she asks, smiling and kissing my hand gently.

"That feeling is how I feel every time I look at you. You simply make me happy." She leans in again and rubs her lips against mine before pressing them against mine.

"I feel the same about you. You have changed me...for the better."

We climb into the luxurious bed. My body instantly sinks into the comfortable bed, suddenly feeling so tired from the day we had. Flying to the white house and meeting the president. We talked *a lot*. It was *exhausting*. She pulls the blankets over us and turns the light off. I snuggle up to her, her arms wrap around me, and I put my leg over hers. Our signature cuddling position.

"Goodnight, honey." She murmurs to me softly.

"Goodnight." I close my eyes and I let out a deep breath, sinking deeper into the soft silk sheets.

Chapter Five: A New Kind of Paradise

"Hey, baby. Get up." Sylvia whispers in my ear. I stir and whine not wanting to oblige. The voice persists. "It's 8 a.m. You must get up."

"NoOo," I whine. I duck under the covers. "I don't wanna!"

She sighs and pulls the covers from me. "Alright, lazy bones. It's time to get up."

"Sylvia," I groan opening my eyes. I come face-to-face with her beautiful face. Her hair is pulled up into a messy bun and I can't help but sit up and pat it. Two strings of hair sit in front of her face, curling down the sides of her jaw. "Pretty," I say in wonderment, still a little out of it from waking up.

"It's time to-" I put a finger against her lips.

"Shhhh. You can't wake me up looking so pretty and not expect me to notice." I grab her shirt, pulling her down.

"Baby, I-" She tries to say but I cut her off with a kiss.

"Come here," I whine, jut my lower lip out, and I open my eyes wide, giving her the puppy dog face.

She sighs. "Okay, but we have to leave soon for-" I pull her back and kiss her more, my finger twirling a little curl that's in front of her face. She climbs on top of me and sits on my lap, her hands cupping my face.

"Such pretty brown eyes," I whisper as I rub my lips against hers.

Her hands move from my cheeks to my long, blonde hair. Her hands massage my scalp all while pushing her body against mine. "They are nothing compared to your emerald gaze. I fight the urge to get lost in your eyes every time I gaze into them. *God,* and your lips...you are so beautiful."

I grip the sides of her shirt as I pull away from her, looking into her eyes. A loud knock on the door breaks our moment. "URGG," I groan rolling my eyes.

She rubs my lower lip with her thumb. My lip's part and she slips her thumb into my mouth. "We'll have more time. I promise." She puts her forehead against mine. I kiss her again not wanting to part.

"Hello?" A voice calls.

"Yeah, yeah. One moment." She looks at me and mouths 'Get dressed.' I dart into the bathroom, and I throw on the clothes I was wearing the day before. I put my shirt and jeans back on and wrap my belt through the belt loops.

I go back outside and watch her talk to someone. That person comes in and starts cleaning the room. "Hello." The lady greets us. "I am the cleaner. I was told that you would be gone by now, and to tidy up. I apologize for intruding."

"No, you're totally fine. We were just getting ready to leave," I say smiling and giving Sylvia side-eye, and biting my lip replaying it in my mind.

She rolls her eyes and returns the lip bite. I walk over to her, and I turn to the cleaner, who is not paying much attention to us. "Okay! Have fun on your little adventure." the cleaning lady says to us.

I lean in and whisper into Sylvia's ear, "Do you have the Chrono Nexus?"

"Yes, I don't know if it would be wise to open it right here."

"Where is a good spot to open a portal to an alternate dimension?"

She smiles. "Good point. Hey, lady! Don't look!" Sylvia says, making us both erupt with laughter. She presses the button on the Chrono Nexus as we continue giggling. We watch in awe as a portal opens in a swirl of bright white. The portal appears to be completely white, so we have no idea what we're stepping into. But alas, it must be done. When we step through, I am surprised by the simplicity of the dimensional change. I thought it would be like spinning in a circle of whiteness like in all the movies you see, but no. We just stepped into the same spot we left like we never left the current time. *Weird.*

"This is going to be a long day," I say to her.

She nods. "Yep! Erin said that there'll be a car called a 'Nebula X?' I don't know what that means. I mean right now it looks normal."

I agree with her, the scenery hasn't changed at all. We walk through the house and open the door. When we do everything changes. I mean *everything.* The world is breathtaking. Picture what a modern, bustling, futuristic city looks like, that is what we're seeing and more. Tall skyscraper buildings with clear roads weaving in between and around them. The amount of greenery is nothing like at home. There are patches of grass all over the entire area, and buildings have huge spaces in between them, instead of being congested in one small area.

"Holy shit!" I blurt out, looking around. I watch as cars speed down the long winding roads, faster than any car at home could go. The sky is bright blue, and the sun shines in the sky, lighting up the verdure Utopolis.

"We should start calling this Utopolis! Utopia and polis!"

"Okay, honey! Instead of saying 'future' we can simply say, 'We are heading to Utopolis!'

I squeal and hop up and down. We walk up to the Nebula X and as I am about to open the door, I realize... "Uh...How do we get in?"

"Greetings, Humans! Are you Sylvia and Natalie?" A voice says. When I look around there is no one.

"Um, hello? Where are you?" Sylvia asks, befuddled.

"I am right in front of you." The voice sounds a little automated, like AI.

"The *car?*" I ask.

"Yes! You *must* be Sylvia and Natalie. Welcome to the future." When the door opens, it appears to have disconnected from the sides of the car, almost as if it's dissolving away.

I get in and look at Sylvia, "What the fuck?!" I exclaim; Because that is all I can say. I am absolutely at a loss for words. The outside of the car looks like a spaceship, it appears to have no windows, and the roof is one piece that curves over the top. The wheels look odd as well. They appear to be built into the sides of the car, melded in. When I step inside, I realize the entire car is one big one-way mirror. We can see out, but nobody can see in. *Zero blind spots here!*

"This, my friend's, is the Nebula X, the only car like it at our time. This is a one-of-a-kind car! Very expensive. Unlike the cars where you come from, all our vehicles are 100% fully electric, and automated. No driver is necessary. This Nebula X 's top speed is 545 mph, which is 195 mph more than the fastest car on Earth. This car has a fully mapped area of the entire world, and the map continuously updates when new roads are built or torn down. New information automatically gets programed into the car, no one needs to manually update the vehicle. It simply scans the local area around it and forms a map that we can understand. This car comes with a full cinematic screen in the back. There's a button in the front of the seat, push it, and see what happens." The Nebula X's AI voice encourages us to do it.

I look over at Sylvia and she makes the 'go ahead' face. I locate the button and press it. I watch as a screen comes out from the top of the car and folds down in front of us. A face appears on the screen, it lacks features other than a mouth and eyes. The AI voice speaks, "Cinema mode activated. What would you like to see?" The face smiles.

"Um..." I think for a moment. "*The War Cry*."

"Now playing '*The War Cry*' on your Synthia. Say 'cancel' anytime to turn off cinema mode or press the button." I watch in amazement as the movie plays, the graphics are astronomical. I can see every single pore and wrinkle on these people's faces. Every individual cell!

"Cancel," I say eager to watch it turn off.

"Cinema mode canceled. Say 'resume' to pick up where you left off, anytime!" The screen folds back into place, almost disappearing into the ceiling.

"What do you think?" The AI asks.

"It's incredible! How did the Stellarborns do this if they were all stupid?" I ask.

"The Astrans helped the Stellarborn species! They showed them the technology and helped them advance swiftly. They also helped come up with some sort of idea to enhance the species' brain waves. They basically copied what the Chrono Nexus did. Except, it didn't change the way they looked, it just reactivated their brain waves!"

"So, they aren't dumb anymore?" I ask.

"Precisely, in a roundabout way."

"Okay, so who is Synthia?" Sylvia interjects.

"Good question, human. Synthia is the AI that controls the car, that would be me! It is sort of like an Alexa® on your Earth, except far less advanced."

I look over at Sylvia and she raises her eyebrows "Wow" she mouths. I nibble on my lower lip, and I widen my eyes. "Wait, where are the seatbelts?"

"Seatbelts are a long-forgotten technology! All cars now are equipped with a state-of-the-art invisible, yet effective electromagnetic field around each passenger's body. When seated, it lets the car know when to activate this technology! Without noticing, it has adjusted itself to help keep you in place, so you don't get harmed in an emergency. The force field detects *any* movement or sudden change in the vehicle's motion! In real-time, it automatically adjusts the intensity and direction, to maintain the balance between safety and comfort. This may happen during acceleration, deceleration, or turns. You can move comfortably in your seat, without worrying about getting out of it! It follows your bodily movements!"

"WHAT?" I yell, looking at Sylvia wide-eyed. She smiles at me and pats my leg.

"That's really cool!" she says, nodding her head.

"Indeed. What's even more impressive, this entire time we were moving at 150 mph, the standard speed limit! In fact, we're here."

"Where is here, exactly?" I ask.

"You're at the entrance of the incredible AstroNova. This is our 'WFSA' if you will. Enjoy the future city of D.C. I am now your designated car! Anytime you need me, I will be here."

We exit the car and look up at the new building. The car drives around and parks in a parking lot designated for AstroNova. I stand and look at the building. The building boasts avant-garde designs, with polished lines and smooth contours that flow indefectibly with the surrounding greenery, and buildings. Glass facades reveal sneak peaks of the bustling activity within the walls, while the exteriors are embellished with holographic displays unveiling the most recent missions and scientific breakthroughs of the community.

The exterior is also embroidered with luminescent lights that jut out in strategic places, scattered around the building. I reach for Sylvia's hands, and she brings my knuckles to her lips and kisses them. "Let's do this shit, baby!" she exclaims, excitedly.

We walk up the graphene staircase and up to the massive door, this door also dissolves when you walk up to it. We're such peasants compared to here.

"Welcome to AstroNova! How can we help you today?" An automated voice says.

I look over to see a robot standing near the door, it looks sort of personish but mechanical. "We're looking for Erin!" I speak.

"Certainly, you must be Sylvia and Natalie! We've been expecting you."

We follow the robot into the heart of the building. The advanced architecture blends seamlessly with sophisticated technology. The roof is dome-like allowing large trees to be planted in the interior adding greenery to balance out the metallic look. We pass many Stellarborns, each looking at us with curiosity, some wave.

"Through the next door on the right is your destination!" The robot, Robo, says. He turns around and walks the other way. Sylvia and I exchange glances before I open the door. The door slides upwards and into the wall.

"Why can't they have normal doors?" I ask Sylvia.

She smiles. "What's a 'normal door?'" She jokes.

I shove her playfully. We step into the office, and the lights blink and illuminate the once-dark room. My eyes wander around, I first observe the walls. These walls are covered in the same pictures and films as the outside of the building had on display. The images flick between different pictures from past endeavors, like a picture frame we have back home. Sitting atop a hovering desk is a translucent screen that shows real-time satellite tracking, telescope observations, exploration missions, and tons of other data that updates 24/7. The furniture is sleek and minimalistic, with a twist of ergonomic chairs and other levitating work areas. Overlooking the city sit some very plush and comfortable looking seats.

I chew on my cheek as I walk around the work area. My eyes catch a glance at Sylvia watching me. "What?" I ask.

She smiles and walks over to me, her hand snakes around my waist.

"Nothing...you just look...so intriguing." She leans in and begins to kiss me when someone interrupts, clearing their throat.

"Excuse me?" A playful voice says.

"Erin!" I gasp and run over to him, hugging him.

"Hey, guys! Good thing I got here when I did...seemed like you two were getting frisky." Erin chuckles and embraces me.

"Not yet!" Sylvia chortles.

I give her another glare when I back away from Erin. She throws her hands up in the air and smiles.

Erin walks over to his seat and plops down in it. "So, do you guys have some good news?"

I sit down in one of the seats, overlooking the scenic view. I turn to face him. "Yes! Both Benjamin and Sebastian have agreed to help us! Sebastian is currently gathering and forming an army!"

"Great! That is *great* news! The Astrans have tried to contact our enemy, but they have yet to tell us why they're here. They have yet to attack, which buys us some time. We did hack into one of their ships and learned they refer to themselves as 'Vorakons.' I'm not gonna lie, it's a nifty name."

I look at Sylvia and nod, agreeing with Erin. She just smirks at me. *She is so obsessed with me.* "That's great! At least we can call them by their actual name. Are the Astrans on a different planet near here?"

He nods. "Yes, they're about five hours and fifty minutes from us! That is roughly how long it would take to get from Earth to Pluto in your time, traveling at light speed."

"Okay...so are we going to go there then?" I ask.

"Yes! We will have to, in order to help the Astrans. I have contacted a large group of Stellarborns to help us fight if it comes to that. We must wait for Sebastian and Benjamin before we can take off as they don't know how to work our technology. It is *far* too advanced."

Sylvia nods and states, "Yes, we got their numbers so they can message us when they're ready."

Erin laughs! "So pure! You can't text them in the future! They're in the past right now! Plus, your phones work using satellites. We don't use satellite imagery or communications."

Sylvia frowns. "Then how will we contact them?"

"I can take care of that! In the meantime, explore the city. Relax for once, it won't kill ya."

He leaves us alone, traveling back in time, I look at Sylvia shocked. "What just happened?"

She shrugs. "I have no idea."

I stand up and do the opposite of relaxing. "We don't know how long this is going to take! We have no idea about any future stuff! We don't know any of these people, we're total outsiders! They think we're a different species! Well, we kind of are! Spieciest! These people are Spieciests!"

Her hands slink around my waist, pulling me against her. She moves my hair to one side and starts, softly, kissing my neck. I close my eyes and reach around, putting my arm around her head. "You need to stop worrying so much." She murmurs in my ear. "We have a car that can tell us *everything*."

I turn around and rest my head against her chest. "I'm sorry," I whisper.

"Don't be, baby. Let's just make the best of this. I mean, we're basically on vacation!"

Chapter Six: Serenity in Utopolis

We climb into the back of our Nebula X and wonder where we should go. "You'll be traveling in space quite frequently, I assume. I suggest going into one of our latest Anti-gravity sports areas! They will go through the basics and what to expect!"

I nod! "Okay! That's fine." I look at Sylvia and she nods.

"Sure! Why not! Take us there Synthia!" Synthia begins driving us through the city, telling us about buildings as we pass them. We both nod along, curiously.

"The statue to your left is of the first Astran to step foot on our land! It was the beginning of a new world for the Stellarborns. Nothing was ever the same!"

"I suppose. I mean the Astrans helped them to develop *all* of this! Even the people in some sort of way." Sylvia says astoundingly.

I put my hand on top of hers, in between us. I realize now that this *is* a vacation for us. Watching her so invested in the history rooted within this city and world is so cute and makes me love her even more.

"We're here!" Synthia says. We both step out of the vehicle and walk into the building. A Stellarborn greets us. "Humans! There has been talk about humans here, but I thought it was just phony talk!"

"Nope! We're here! We're looking to do some flying. What do you call it?"

"Anti-gravity Sports?"

"Yes! That!" She smiles and I can't help but giggle.

"Wonderful! Someone will be with you shortly to show you the ropes."

"Do we have to pay...or?" I question, raising my eyebrows.

The Stellarborn laughs. "No! You are guests in our world! We welcome you! Besides, your money is worthless to us!"

I look at Sylvia and nod, sticking my lower lip out, impressed. I lean in and whisper in her ear, "I think I could get used to this whole 'important people' thing."

She laughs and nods agreeingly, squinting her eyes.

"Alright, Ladies," A male voice begins. "I am Ethan, and I will be your tour guide. I will show you the basics of space travel and what to do in some situations!" I nod and follow him, Sylvia next to me. "Now this is a high-tech virtual reality simulation. None of what you see, or feel is real. It is merely a type of virtual reality that instead of needing to wear goggles, or something of the sort, you can taste, feel, hear, and see whatever you want. In this simulation, we're going to experiment with microgravity. This is the first thing everyone going in space must adapt to."

We step into a bright white room and at first, I feel normal until suddenly everything changes, and we're transported into space. My body begins to feel as if it's hovering and at first, I feel fine, but then I realize I don't know how to move. I begin to panic, looking around trying to find Sylvia. "Relax." I hear a voice whispering to me from my left. "Remember, it's just a simulation. It's not real. Focus on where you are. Take in your surroundings."

I look around, noticing hand bars on the spaceship. I grab them and begin pulling myself in the direction of the noise. "Good, follow my voice." I continue pulling myself in that direction until I see Sylvia floating in the spaceship, holding onto a bar. I bite my lip as I drag myself to her. She launches herself at me, wrapping her arms around me, and we start floating in the air together. "You did so well." She whispers to me, softly. I rub my lips against hers and I smile.

"Thank you." As soon as we part, the simulation turns off. I instantly feel wobbly, almost falling to the ground but Sylvia was still holding onto me.

"Well done!" Ethan says, clapping his hands. "That was excellent teamwork you did by communicating with each other, to guide yourselves to each other. Teamwork is a huge part of the deal when you're in space! You must rely on others to keep safe. When you land on the ground and do get gravity, it will be a shock to your muscles. In space, your muscles degrade the longer you're up because they don't have to do as much work."

We look at each other and nod. "Wonderful! Lesson two: radiation exposure. On your Earth and ours, radiation exposure is less of an issue! This is because of the 'Ozone layer.' The Ozone layer is made merely of Ozone molecules or 'O3' molecules. This happens in the stratosphere, the second layer of Earth's atmosphere. How this works is oxygen molecules or 'O2 molecules' are struck with Ultraviolet radiation. This breaks apart the O2 molecules. These lone molecules combine to form O3 molecules."

He continues. "This reaction absorbs most of the Ultraviolet rays! The ones that get through, usually UV-B and UV-C, bounce from the ocean, water, snow, sand, and other reflective surfaces. In contrast, the Earth's surface soaks in UV rays. Dark surfaces, such as dirt: the darker the surface usually the more UV rays it soaks in, or they soak into plants for photosynthesis. Humans wear sunscreen to protect themselves from this phenomenon! The significance to this is when you *leave* the Ozone Layer, you're no longer protected by it. Astronauts must take precautions to protect themselves from it."

He snaps his finger and *bam* we're back in 'space.' "Now for a more visual lesson. One way to keep track of your radiation exposure is something called a 'Dosimeter.' If you look at your arm, you'll notice there is what looks like a thermostat!

This is your personal Dosimeter. The red bar shows how much radiation you have encountered! The higher the bar is, the more detrimental the situation. These are also scattered inside your spacecraft to measure the average radiation in the ship! Dosimeters are over a period of time though, so they're not as accurate as 'Active Radiation Monitoring.'"

He presses some buttons on the screen in front of us and shows us how much *active radiation* we are currently consuming. "Active Radiation Monitoring tracks, in real-time, how much radiation you are *currently* consuming. This is much more effective than a Dosimeter since Dosimeters just give you a general analysis. Passive vs. Active radiation systems! Knowing this is not as noteworthy since our aircraft and even yours are designed to reflect radiation waves! These devices are more needed *outside* of the aircraft."

He gets out of the seat in front of the craft and guides us over to a closet. "Now, one of the *most* important parts of space travel is your space suit and knowing the precautions for life support." He grabs a spherical tube that connects to the back of all the space suits. "Air supply is crucial, no atmosphere no air. No air, you're shit outta luck." We chuckle at that. "This is why you *always* must have an oxygen tank on you *and* to make sure to fill it when it nears empty. All our aircraft have a designated filling area. You just put the nozzle in the hole." He shows us the hole and slips the nozzle inside. "And push a button. It'll beep when it is full. You get two tanks to further prevent you from suffocation! Your suit also protects from extreme temperatures and micrometeoroids!"

He walks down the belly of the aircraft and directs us to an air vent. "The vents are dispersed around the aircraft. When you exhale you release carbon dioxide into the air. This won't leave the air in the aircraft, so these vents push it out into space! Oxygen vents also circulate the aircraft, these only turn on at cruising speeds. Next is temperature regulation. Just like in a house, the aircraft is designed to maintain a comfortable temperature. This works using heaters, radiators, and insulation materials."

I finally come up with a question. "What about food and water?"

"Wonderful segway into my next conversation! The food we bring is enough to last for the entire journey, we try to pack *more* than necessary to ensure starvation doesn't happen. As with water, you're given a strict amount of water and a filtration system to ensure clean drinking water."

I cringe. "Filtering...pee?"

He nods and smiles. "Precisely. To get into space and where you need to go, the aircraft can't exceed a certain weight. This ensures that it won't! The filtration is excellent! You won't even know the difference!"

After *many* hours of going over orbital mechanics, psychological challenges, communication techniques, emergency procedures, and crew cohesion we finally leave. By now it is nearing eight p.m. and we're both exhausted and starving. When we get in the car it takes us to a local restaurant that has similar foods to what we eat at home.

After another hour of eating, our car drives us to a hotel. This hotel is in the sky, *floating* in the sky. I would be freaking out if I wasn't so fricking tired. We walk into the hotel and are greeted by more Stellarborns. They direct us to our extremely fancy room, again free of cost. I take my shirt off, unbuckle my belt as I strip my pants off and dive face-first into the bed.

"Is my baby tired?" Sylvia asks as she climbs next to me, her shirt and pants sitting on the floor next to mine.

I nod. "So tired. I didn't realize how much shit we had to worry about." I sit up and look at her, my eyes half-lidded.

She tucks a strand of hair behind my ear and offers a sweet smile. "You did so good though." She whispers. She gets closer to me, her finger trailing down my arm, softly. I let out a soft sigh and I rest my forehead against hers, putting my hand on the back of her head.

"So did you," I whisper back barely audible.

"Let's lay down, baby girl." We climb into the core of the bed and rest our heads against the pillow. "Apparently, Utopolis still favors beds and pillows to something more future-y."

She giggles. "Mhm, I suppose." She claps her hands, and the lights dim and then shut off. She pulls the blankets over us and runs her finger down my jaw.

"Can we spoon today?" I ask against her lips.

"Of course, do you want to be the big or little spoon?"

I gasp. "Obviously little."

"I had to ask!" She remarks. I turn around and push into her as she wraps her arms around me, her leg climbing into between mine. I let out another content sigh as I close my eyes.

"Goodnight, baby." She whispers in my ear. Her hand caresses my side so gently I can barely feel it. Her hand lands on my side, gripping it gently.

After what feels like hours but, was only 10 or so minutes, I can't fall asleep. "Sylvia...are you awake?" I whisper.

"Yes," a faint voice replies. "Are you okay?"

"I can't fall asleep."

"Do you want to chitchat a little bit?" Her hand moves up and down my thigh, softly stroking it as she speaks.

"Mhm," I murmur.

"Turn around for me." I rotated around to face her. She instantly pulls me closer, keeping her leg tucked between mine. "Did you have something in mind?"

I nod but remember she can't see me. "Yes," I begin. "Have you ever thought about consciousness?"

"What do you mean?" I nuzzle my head into the crook of her neck. She lets out a soft sigh as I nibble on her earlobe.

"The fact that we exist. We're here right now. Living. Conscious. I just think it is a little odd to think about sometimes."

She turns her head to look at me, her lips so close to mine. "Have you ever thought about how we're about to meet an actual Alien race? I have always believed in Aliens, but I guess we were too primitive to see them."

"I love Aliens. I think that Aliens are so cool. Except I don't understand why humans make them out to be evil...maybe we're the only evil ones?"

She shakes her head against me. "Don't forget about *why* we're going to meet this species, baby. Remember the Vorakons? They're Alien to us but they're not good."

I run my hand down her jaw. "That's where you're wrong. From *our point of view,* we see them as warmongers. That doesn't mean they are. Who knows what could have happened in the past that the Astrans haven't mentioned? Maybe, the Astrans have some secrets they don't wanna share with us."

"Mmmm, I never thought about it like that. Perhaps you're right?" She finds my hand and intertwines her fingers with mine.

"It's so refreshing when you don't dismiss my ideas. You make me feel valued and heard." I say, leaning even closer to her, wanting to be nearer to her.

"Why would I ever dismiss your ideas? Your perspective is important to me, and we're a team," she replies, her words strike an emotional chord within my body, causing tears to well up in the corners of my eyes and trickle down my cheeks. "Are you crying?" she asks with concern, releasing my hand and placing a gentle finger on my cheek. "Baby, what's wrong? Did I say something hurtful?"

Her tenderness only makes me cry more, her understanding and love touches me like always. "No, you said everything perfectly. You're just so perfect." I managed to blurt out through tears.

"I don't understand. Then why are you crying?" Her voice is charged with genuine concern. It's so hard to control my emotions when she talks so softly and nicely. Something I am not used to.

"I've never met anyone like you. You…" I pause, taking in a deep breath. I sit up and she reaches over to tap the lamp and gently irradiates the room.

"What is it?" she whispers. She drags her index finger across my jaw as she scopes out my features, trying to find something in them, a crack in my barrier. Her gaze trails down my body, her lower lip being captured by her teeth.

"I-" The way she is looking at me is making it so hard to focus on what I was about to say. She leans closer to me, retracing my jaw with her lips. When she pulls back slightly, she pushes my head back with her hand. She moves down to my neck, planting small, loving kisses on my throat. "Sylvia," I question, my hands running up and down her back, my eyes fluttering closed. I know what she's doing. She's trying to force my guard down and I just might.

"Don't let me distract you." She smiles as I tilt my head back down to meet her gaze.

I continue from where I left off as she draws circles on the palm of my hand. *Honesty.* "I have never had anyone that truly understands me the way you do. You listen, support, and care for me more than anyone has. Your kindness, intelligence, and empathy are all a sharp contrast to my previous relationships. It's new for me to be treated with such respect, tender love, and care."

She kneels in front of me, sitting on her legs, and reaches for my hand, guiding me to her height. I look at her, curiously, to know what she's up to. "I want you to listen to every word when I say this to you, okay?" I nod my head and look down, reaching for her hands. She intertwines our fingers and whispers, "Look at me, baby." I look back up at her, tears already retracing their previous steps. "I am not a past relationship, I am not going to use you to just say I have a girlfriend or for sex. I am *with* you through thick and thin...better or worse." Tears begin to spill down her cheeks now and it makes my heart hurt seeing her cry. "I would *never* do anything to purposely hurt, disrespect, or disregard your feelings." My head begins to tilt down but she lets go of one of my hands and tilts my head back up. "I know it's hard for you to believe me, but I will show you. Okay?"

I move closer to her and sit back down on my legs. "You already have. From being here with me right now to saving my life the first time you even saw me...even kissing me that first time. It was magical...your touch is so soft, so tender. Your lips were enchanting and your voice, oh my God." I throw my head back remembering the moment we shared. I rise from my legs, my face hovering over her. "Your eyes glistened under the setting moon and the flickering of the fire. *Your beautiful brown eyes.* I got to see details I had never gotten close enough to see, I got to see your little brown freckles that I love so much. They're so pretty, the first time I saw them, in that moment, I couldn't help but touch them. Your skin was so soft. Do you remember?"

"Yes, baby. I do." She whispers as she looks up at me, her brows furrowed. "Your touch was so delicate, so inviting."

I nod and smile. "In that moment I couldn't help but allow my eyes to fall to your lips." I capture my lower lip between my teeth thinking about hers. "I had wanted to kiss you on the plane! I didn't though and I am so glad I didn't. That moment you whispered 'please' with your lips so close to mine, I couldn't resist, it made my knees weak. I gave in and God was it worth it. Did you feel it when we kissed? It felt like I was struck by lightning, in the most incredible way ever. It felt as if the entire world stopped in its tracks and it was just us...spinning around on this massive rock, we were alone and I loved it, I never wanted it to stop."

She rises up to her hind legs and pulls me into her by my waist. "I remember. I remember it like it was yesterday. I was craving it so badly. So, *fucking* badly. After the day we had it was absolutely perfect. The lighting, the tension, and you. I re-play it in my head every single time I look at you. The way your skin looked under the moonlit sky; I could have sworn I saw it shimmer. Your eyes were so astonishing as well. That very first day I met you when you looked into my eyes, I was gone. I knew you were the one. I knew I wanted you. *You're so beautiful.*"

"Really?" I ask, astonished, not wanting her to stop.

"Yes. The way you looked at me...like I stopped your heart. Like your little mind was going a mile a minute trying to process everything, then you looked at me and it was like someone flipped a switch and you didn't care anymore. About your job, the 'asteroid,' or your coworker. It was beautiful. I wanted to kiss you right then and there. You looked like you needed it. Like no one had looked at you the way I did...ever. I didn't just want to kiss you then though, in fact, every time I looked at you, I wanted to kiss you. I knew you felt the same, I could tell. Every time I'd look at you, you'd blush and get all antsy."

"I couldn't help it. When you looked at me it felt like you had stripped away the wall, I built around myself...it felt as if I was naked around you...vulnerable."

"Who hurt you, baby? Why did you build a wall around yourself? Why did it scare you to be vulnerable with me?"

I look down taking a deep breath, wondering if I should tell her this. "It's...a lot," I whisper.

"I understand if you aren't comfortable telling me but remember...I will never judge you or disregard anything you tell me." I chew on the inside of my cheek and look back up at her.

"There was this girl," I begin. "I met her after my second transfer. We lived close to each other and went to school together. We became friends, instantly. We really hit it off. It was in seventh grade; we were so young...she was a year older than me in eighth grade. She suggested we experiment...I said no. I wasn't comfortable with my sexuality yet and I didn't like her like that. She was pissed. She called me all sorts of words. 'You're such a *bitch!* It's not even a big deal!' she had said. She stormed out of my house and of course, my mom didn't even notice. She was doing whatever drug she could get her hands on. We never talked after that. I was alone."

I sigh. "After I graduated high school...what...? I am twenty-five right now...so seven years ago. *Damn.* Anyway, I met her at a bar, we were both tipsy and one thing led to another...we went to my place. Afterwards in the morning, I got her number. We started going out more, I really liked her but soon after we started dating it got... physically and emotionally abusive. At first, it was small things, you know. Telling me what I can and can't wear. Telling me who I could spend time with. I thought it was endearing but then it got worse. If I did something wrong, she'd yell at me, tell me I am pathetic, she would tell me that no one would love me because I always screw everything up."

I cover my face with my hands, and I begin to sob. I have never told anyone this and now that I finally am, I realize how hurt it has made me. My body trembles from crying so hard. Sylvia rests my head on her chest and runs her hands through my hair. Finally, I speak again, "One day." I Look up at her. "One day, I forgot to take the trash out like she asked me to do. She yelled, then she hit me. She slapped me across the face. I had a bruise on my face for weeks. After she hit me, she instantly apologized, and I thought it was okay. I thought it would get better. She started to change and started to praise me instead. I thought we could work it out..."

Sylvia offers a weak smile, encouraging me to continue. So, I do. "Then it started again. She started name-calling and making herself the victim. Telling me that *I'm* the problem. She did this so much, I started to believe her. I walked on eggshells around her, trying to make sure I didn't mess up, like I always do and get yelled at or hit. I thought I loved her. It's like a mix of starving man syndrome and Stockholm syndrome. I was starved for love and attention, and felt kidnapped in the situation I was in. I felt like I couldn't leave because no one else would love me the way she did...or the way I thought she did. Sometimes, I still feel as if it was my fault."

Sylvia looks broken. Tears are streaming down her cheeks, and I didn't notice but she is also shaking. "I'm so sorry," she says barely audible. She wipes the tears from her cheeks and takes a deep breath. Fanning her face with her hand. "Shit." She chuckles but not because she thinks it's funny. "First of all. Number one in abusive relationships: *never* blame the victim. It is *never* the victim's fault. What she did to you was *not* okay." She grits her teeth as she says it. She is pissed. "That is what abusers do, baby. They use your feelings. They build tension in the relationship and start controlling what you do, and/or who you see. They make you feel bad if you want to hang out with other people. 'You always hang out with your friends; we never see each other.' They draw you away from those you care about, so you don't go to others for advice. To trap you."

She proceeds. "Next stage is an incident like you said. This can be physical, emotional, verbal, or sexual abuse. Then they act sorry. 'I'll never do it again' they might say. Then it'll relax. Start to feel better until tension builds again and the cycle repeats. They degrade you and make you feel unworthy of another's love. Make you feel like what you have now is the best you'll get, or the only thing you'll get. They might even say it's normal." I lean up and kiss her, my hands cupping her face. She lets out a 'huh' noise. "What...?" She whispers as I part.

"Thank you," I whisper against her lips. "You're the only person I have ever told that to...the only person that cared enough to listen."

"How did you get out of it?"

I sigh. "At the time we lived in an apartment and there was, what you called, an 'incident.' She hit me again, a lot of times. My whole face was bruised. She broke my nose, busted my lip, and was screaming at me. I guess someone next door called the police, and they caught her in the act. I was laying on the floor, my body was numb. I couldn't move. They brought me to the hospital, and I guess arrested her for domestic abuse. That was my realization that what she had been doing to me wasn't okay. If those people didn't intervene...I could be dead right now."

"I am so grateful that you can be here with me right now. I am so glad you realized that what she was doing was wrong. You deserve all the love in the world. I promise you that." I smile at her words, and I nod.

"Me too," I mutter. I crawl back under the sheets, and she joins me. "Thank you for talking with me about this."

"I am always here to listen to you, Natalie. Always." I cuddle up next to her and I begin to close my eyes. "Goodnight," she murmurs.

"Goodnight," I murmur back. She pulls me closer. I finally feel at ease with what happened. Maybe now I can finally start to heal from what happened to me. Maybe I finally start to move on from what those girls did to me. All thanks to Sylvia. I owe so much to her.

Chapter Seven: Exploring Utopolis

"Come on! We must go clothes shopping!" I call out to Sylvia.

"I am going as fast as I can, honey!" She calls back. I tap my finger impatiently against my thigh. I guess this is what we get for not packing *anything*. She emerges from the bathroom and walks over to me at the door leading into the hallway. "Finally," I exasperate.

"Oh, shut up!" She snickers. She puts her arm over my shoulder as we walk out of the room and lock it.

"See ya!" The front desk agent calls. We nod at the woman and disappear out of the hotel. We walk down the steps and turn towards the parking lot. We spot our car and walk over to it.

"I love our car," I say as we step in.

"Greetings, Humans! I am glad you like me! I do my best!" Synthia says. "Where to?"

"We're looking for a clothing store, does Utopolis have them?" Sylvia asks.

"Of course, you'll have to visit a tailor though. No clothing stores have clothes for humans!"

"Right...then we'd like to go to the nearest tailor shop," She responds and chuckles.

The car roars to life and we begin to move out of the parking lot and down the translucent roads. "Can we listen to a song?" I ask.

Both the car and Sylvia say, "Yes, what would you like to listen to?"

I look at Sylvia wide-eyed. "Sheesh, maybe you should date the car."

She gasps, shoves my shoulder, and laughs. "Oh my God, Natalie."

I shrug and ask the car to play some pop music. I look at her as I dance and sing along to several of the songs. I grab her hand and swing her arm back and forth, bobbing my head up and down. She laughs at me and starts singing with me, matching my vibe. "Get it! Get it! Get it!" I hype her up and laugh with her.

"Sorry to intrude but you have arrived at your destination!" Synthia interrupts. We both exit the car and looked up at the tailoring shop.

"This is gonna suck," I blurt out and look at Sylvia.

"Yep!" She agrees. We head into the store and are greeted by someone.

"Welcome to Jame's Tailoring Shop! What can I do for you?"

I watch Sylvia approach the desk. "Hello! We're looking for a whole new wardrobe. For both of us. We forgot our clothes in the past."

"Yeah, you know casually forgot to pack for the future. Nothing too crazy." I lean on the counter and look at Sylvia smirking.

She laughs at me. "What she said." The front desk person laughs.

"Alright. I assume you came here because you're humans?"

"Good eye," Sylvia shoots back.

"Right this way." She guides us to a room and asks one of us to stand on the pedestal in the center of the room. "This scans your body, and perfectly estimates your size for any clothing item, including bras and underwear!" I stand on the podium and watch a screen in front of me turn on. A reflection of my naked body appears on the screen and my eyes widen.

"Oh my God!" I cry out.

I look at Sylvia who just raises her eyebrows and nods. "Uh-huh." She smirks.

"It's okay, I won't look. It'll go away eventually."

"Awe," Sylvia whines. "Is there a way to make it stay?"

"Sylvia!" I yell, scolding her.

She throws her hands up "Hey! It's not my fault, you're the naked one, not me."

"Whatever." I roll my eyes.

"Calculations completed!" the monitor embedded into the wall says. The screen begins to show hundreds of outfits that match my body type and my form.

"Wonderful! Now you can just click on the different items you'd like, and it'll be made instantaneously and free of charge." On the pillar I am standing on, a translucent screen floats up from the ground and spins to face me. I begin swiping upward on the screen and look at the clothing options.

"Mmmm, you should definitely do this one," Sylvia suggests pointing to a black V-cut shirt that dips...very low. "It would...bring out your eyes."

I raise my eyebrows at her, and I click on it and add it to my cart. I smirk at her when she pounds her fist in the air for a celebratory victory. I roll my eyes and continue picking out shirts, bras, underwear, pants, shorts, crop tops, shoes, and socks. When I finish, I click *complete,* and I walk over to this area that says 'pick-up.' When it finishes several intricate boxes come out of the slot and in front of me.

I grab them as they come out and set them down next to the shoot. I look at Sylvia, a tired look in my eyes. *So many clothes to unpack urg.* "Well, I'll leave you two to it! Give me a holler if you need help!" She leaves and goes back to her work area.

"Now it's *your* turn." I bite my lip and I look at the screen as she stands on the podium. When I look at her, she is blushing.

"Uh-huh, not so fun when it's you, is it?" I gestured for her to lean down and when she does, I kiss her. "I'm just teasing, baby." She smiles at me and kisses me again.

"Please stand upright for concise calculations," The AI screen commands.

"You heard her." I tease. She rolls her eyes and huffs a breath through her lips. She stands upright and waits impatiently for it to finish.

"Calculations completed!" I squeal and observe the clothing items. We collaborate on clothes for her until she finally presses 'complete.'

It starts spitting out her clothing and when it's done, we each must carry three large boxes full of clothes out of the store. We didn't know how much we'd need so we ordered several months' worth of clothes. We haul them to the car and by the time we get there I'm panting trying to catch my breath. "These boxes are *heavy!*" I wheeze. She pats my back and chortles.

"Indeed, I can put them in the trunk, honey. You sit down." I sit down in the backseat like I always have, and I close my eyes.

"Welcome!" Synthia greets us as Sylvia steps in.

"Hello, Synthia! We'd like to go back home to unpack our clothing," I speak.

"Certainly, would you like to resume your music?" Synthia asks.

I shake my head. "No, I just wanna chill."

"Understood." She starts to drive us home, allowing me to look over at Sylvia and let out a deep breath.

"I know," she whispers. "Come to me." I get closer to her, letting her arms embrace me. I close my eyes and I take a long, deep breath. "When we get home, you can take a little nap if you want."

I look up at her. "No, I don't wanna put all the stress on your shoulders," I whisper.

She runs her hands through my hair and kisses me tenderly. "Letting you sleep while I put clothes away is not a stressor for me, baby girl."

"Kiss me again," I murmur. My eyes remain closed as she leans down and kisses me again. Her lips move in sync with mine. "I am already so exhausted," I whimper.

"I know, baby," she whispers back. "Sit on my lap." I climb on her lap. My legs are tucked next to hers. I rest my head on her shoulder as her hands massage my scalp. "My sleepy girl," she purrs in my ear. I nuzzle her neck and let out a soft sigh.

"You have arrived at your destination," Synthia says.

"I keep forgetting how fast these cars are," I groan. Synthia laughs at me. I climb off Sylvia, and I groan, remembering all those boxes. "Dreaded boxes. Why can't they make shit teleport?"

She grabs my hand and places her other on my cheek. "It'll be okay. Once we get these boxes inside, you can take a power nap."

I nod my head and I embrace her. We walk over to the already-opened trunk. I grab boxes, stacking two on top of me. I begin to walk inside and into our room. Luckily, we're on the first floor. I walk to our room number, and I put my face into the face scanner.

"Access granted." The door says and the door opens by itself. I walk in and set boxes near the bed. When I walk out, I see Sylvia coming so I keep the door open for her.

"Thank you, baby. I can take care of the last two boxes." I shake my head.

"I get one and you get one." She smiles at me, and we walk out, the door closes. We grabbed one and then tap the button to close the trunk. The car goes and parks as we walk away. We walk back to the room. Face ID and then:

"Access Granted." We step in and set the rest of the boxes near the bed. I sit onto the bed and close my eyes. She rubs my back gently and kisses my shoulder.

"Get some rest, baby," her soft voice whispers into my ear. I position myself vertically on the bed, my head against the pillows. She pulls the covers over me and kisses my forehead. I close my eyes and instantly fall asleep.

"**A**re you still asleep?" A soft voice mumbles into my ear.

"Mm?" I question turning to them and wrapping my arms around them, knowing who it is. When she doesn't resist, I know it's Sylvia.

"I didn't mean to wake you, baby." Her hands run up and down my sides, as she rubs her cheek against the top of my head.

"Mm." I open my eyes and turn my head to look at her.

"Hello, beautiful girl." She tucks strands of hair behind my ear and soothingly rubs my cheek with her hand. I grab her hand and I hug it. I strain my neck to kiss her, my lips caressing hers. She leans down and delicately pushes me down. She continues to kiss me, soft sighs and whimpers escaping both of our lips.

"What time is it?" I wonder.

"Dinner time. I came to wake you up to see if you were hungry." I look up at her and I smile.

"How long was I asleep?"

"Only five hours."

"*Five hours!?*" I say flabbergasted. "I'm sorry, baby." I pout, sitting up. She pushes me back down and runs her hand down my arm.

"Don't be. I enjoyed watching you sleep."

"You watched me for five hours?" I whisper.

She bites her lip. "No, only three. It was a lot of clothes...and I got distracted sometimes."

"You're wearing our new clothes." My eyes travel up and down her body.

"Do you like it?" She smirks.

I nod. "More than like. Is it comfortable?"

"Yes. It fits so snugly." I begin to sit up again, and I rub the fabric in between my index finger and thumb.

"It looks so good on you." I crawl on her lap, and I straddle her. "And to answer your question. I am hungry."

"What does my baby want?" She strokes my cheek as she looks at me, smiling.

"You know I'm not good at making decisions," I pout.

"Let's go talk to Synthia, and see what's around, okay?"

I smile and nod. We walk out of the room and stroll to our car. When we get in, Synthia greets us. "Hello! Where to?"

"We were trying to figure out where to eat for dinner!"

"Well, there's a restaurant called 'PixelPlates.' It is completely powered by AI and 3D printing technology."

I widen my eyes and look at Sylvia. "Like, food? They 3D print food?"

"Precisely. Climate Change was getting out of hand, and the Astrans showed them their technologies for overcoming the barrier."

"Barrier?" Sylvia asks.

"Ah! Let's dive into some cool stuff guys. Listen to this. In this lesson, we're going to cover 'The Fermi Paradox.' The observable universe is roughly nighty billion light years in diameter. There are one hundred billion galaxies, each holding one hundred to one billion stars. Within these universes are millions of trillions of planets that are *also* habitable. With the technology you all have, you're limited to the local group. Space expands, and it is *still* expanding as we speak. With *our* technology, we jumped millions of years in the future because of the Astrans. We have a much *larger* 'local group.'"

"The Milky Way, our galaxy, has up to four-hundred billion stars, there are roughly twenty billion sun-like stars as well. In a solar system, the planet must be a certain distance away to be habitable. $\frac{1}{5}$ of these solar systems have this. Now, let's talk about types of civilizations. Type one: They can access the full energy available on their planet. That being fusion, natural elements, renewable, and resources such as coal. This is where you all are. Type two civilizations can harness the power of their sun! This is called a Dyson sphere. Finally, type three. This is a very advanced civilization that can control its entire galaxy and energy."

Synthia laughs. "Enough background! It's time. You humans probably wonder 'Why can't we see Aliens?' Am I right?"

"Yes," I say, excitedly.

"Welcome to The Fermi Paradox. Filters. A filter, in this context, is a barrier that prohibits life from passing by easily. Now, let me tell you what you humans believe, you either have passed them, the filters are ahead of you all, or it doesn't exist, and you humans are alone. So sad...you all wanna know the truth?"

"Yes!" Sylvia says.

"The filters exist, but you all are nowhere near passing them. Your species is such a feeble-minded species, with such bad communication, and reasonable thinking, other species laugh in your demise. They throw pity at you. You all get excited to see our ships! We chose to show you those ships! Where you are in the past. You can't see us because we are so ahead of your time, our ships go faster than the speed of light, and faster than any of your cameras or eyes could detect. People are so worked up about figuring out if Climate Change is real, they don't ever sit down and discuss science."

I look down at my hands. I know Synthia is right. Humans suck. "What does this have to do with Climate Change?"

"Climate Change is the first barrier. If a civilization can't pass such a barrier, civilization dies. Meat is a huge issue. On average one cow yields 155 pounds of meat. As of 2021, there were 93,789.5 cows. Assuming all the cows are the same, which they aren't, but theoretically, that is 14.5 billion pounds (about 6.5 billion kg) of meat for cows. In 2021, the United States alone held 326.7 million people. In the United States, 30 billion pounds (about 13.6 billion kg) of beef was consumed. To put that in perspective, that is about 2,000 fully grown elephants or 90 Olympic-sized pools. The average African Elephant can weigh between 5,000-14,000 pounds (about twice the weight of an elephant) and the average Olympic pool can carry 660,000 gallons (about 2.4 million L) of water."

My eyes widen as I look at Sylvia. "This is an issue *because* not all animals are treated with respect, eating so much meat is bad for you, it can clog arteries, especially beef, cause cancers, and perhaps irregular bowel movements, dehydration, and tying into this conversation, 124.7 million acres (about twice the area of Arizona) of land is used to produce cattle, this includes crop land to feed them. This is 41% of the United States land, as of 2021. Why is this bad? Greenhouse gas emissions, deforestation land use and water consumption, water pollution, feed production, energy intensity, waste management, and biodiversity loss."

"I don't understand the feed production and energy intensity issues. What's wrong with the first one and what does 'energy intensity' mean?" I ask.

"To produce feed for cattle they must build feed productions, to transport them they need to use cars, to process them, they must take them to processing plants. Feed production is part of those 124.7 million acres of land. Some of their food, for example, soybeans. They require 19 inches of rain to grow 85 bushels.

Doesn't seem like much? That could fill almost two 55-gallon rain barrels. In 2021, 4.44 billion bushels of soybeans were produced. Math time." Synthia pauses, most likely figuring out the math. "First, we must divide the number of inches, 19, by the number of bushels 19 inches would make. That is 85. This will equal .2235 inches per bushel. Now let's multiply that by 4.44 billion which will equal 992,076,000 inches of water. Converting this to gallons, it would take 3.88 trillion gallons (about 14.6 trillion L) of water to produce this."

I rub my head with my hands, and I look at Sylvia. "Wow."

She nods. "Let's go try some 3D-printed food!"

"If you'd like, every topic can be different when you get into your car!"

I nod. "Yes, I quite like these conversations, do you Sylvia?"

"Yeah. They're interesting, really."

We step out of the car and into the restaurant. Instantly, we're greeted with AI.

"How many?" A robot asks.

"Two," Sylvia replies.

"Right this way, Ladies," Robo says. We follow Robo to a booth table. We look for the menus until we watch as they hover from inside of the table, floating up towards us. These menus are also translucent and show all the foods the same way a paper menu would. The look of this restaurant has a mix of modern and futuristic characteristics. The walls are that of waves, swooping across the walls to perceive motion. The floors are an interesting wood-like material, that spans the width of the restaurant. Sprawled out in the guts of the restaurant are high tables and stools, a bar, along regular height chairs, like our Earth. The booths light up purple when people are seated in them. "I assume you're new to this, so if you have any questions, you have a button near your table to request help. Just click on foods on the menu and when you're done ordering you click 'order.' It's as simple as that. Can I get you started on some drinks?"

I look at the menu and squint my eyes trying to understand the drink menu. I read the description for 'laser lemonade.' A tangy lemonade with a twist of ginger and a dashing of sparkling lemon-flavored water served on the rocks with a lemon wheel. "I'll get the laser lemonade." I smile. *Look at me trying new things.*

"I'll do the Sonic Sunset, please, and thank you." Sylvia smiles and I can't help but grin at her. When the waiter leaves Sylvia looks at me. "Why you got that grin on your face."

I sigh happily. "I am just happy."

She leans over the table. "Why is that?"

"You. This. Us." I look at my menu and chew on my cheek, trying to figure out what to get. "We get appetizers?" I ask.

"If you'd like. I am down."

"Can we do the 'Quantum Queso Dip?'"

I watch as she reads the blurb, velvety cheese dip infused with pixelated peppers, served with crispy binary tortilla chips. "Yes! I am down for that."

I squeal happily, people look at us like we're idiots. *I'm sorry it's cool we're eating literal homemade food!* It's quite literally homemade. Everything. "I know what I am gonna get," I say.

"What's that?"

"The 'CyberCow Ribeye.' 3D-printed ribeye steak with immersive augmented reality sauce, served with pixelated mashed potatoes."

"I was going for the 'TechnoTerra Tofu Steak.' Locally sourced pixel-printed tofu, marinated and seared to perfection, combined with data-driven vegetable medley."

"*Damn*! We are going to be eating well today. Gotta love 'locally sourced pixel-printed tofu." She laughs at me and rolls her eyes.

"This place has got some jokes, doesn't it?"

"Indeed. Will we want a dessert?" I ask.

"We could share the 'DataDessert Trio.' A trio of mini desserts showcasing pixel artistry, incorporating data-driven tarts, pixel mousse, and *byte*-sized confections."

"Yeah! That's good!" I agree.

We click order and I am prompted with *How long do you want your main course to be delivered to you after your appetizer?* "How long do you think it'll take for us to eat our appts?" I question.

"Mmm." She thinks. "Fifteen minutes maybe?"

I nod. "I'll have them bring the main courses out twenty minutes after appetizers are served."

"What about desserts? Half an hour, maybe?"

"Yeah, that's fine." I bob my head up and down.

"Perfect, done!" she exclaims.

"Me too!" Within seconds, our food appears out of the table. Literally comes out on a pedestal. I look at her, mouth ajar.

"What?" she asks amazed. When it comes out, it looks like regular chips with a white cheesy dip.

"That just happened." We begin to dig into the food, and it surprisingly tastes exactly like normal chips and queso dip! "It's delicious!"

"Yes! I agree. I could really get used to this."

"We'll have to go back to the past. No!" I say elongating the 'o' sound. When we finish, the dish is automatically brought back onto the table.

She smiles at me as she rests her chin on the palm of her hand.

"What?" I ask, crossing my arms.

"You have a little bit of queso on the corner of your mouth. She gestures to herself and points to where it is on me. "Other side."

"Did I get it?"

She shakes her head. "Come here." I lean forward and she swipes it off my face, using a napkin.

"Thanks," I murmur, blushing slightly.

"What's with the pretty blush?" she asks, smirking.

I look down. "It's a little embarrassing."

"Why? I don't mind. I find it endearing."

This only makes me blush more. I look at her, cringing at myself. She begins to lean over the table, but our main courses come up. I catch the little sigh she exhales from her nose. I grab my plate and I observe my steak and mashed potatoes. Once again, the food is exquisite. "Want a bite?" I ask.

She nods. I begin with the potatoes, scooping some up on the spoon and feeding it to her. Her eyes widen "Mmm!"

I scoop some up and taste it. "It's so good!"

I cut into my steak and feed it to her. Her eyes widen and she groans. After she swallows, she says, "It's delicious!"

She starts feeding me her food and I have the same reactions as she did. "This food is almost better than the majority of restaurants in our world!"

"Utopolis really is incredible."

We walk out of the restaurant and go over to Synthia. "Greetings! How was your meal?"

"Oh my God!" we both say in unison and then laugh.

"It was so good!" Sylvia confirms.

"I am pleased to hear that! Where to next?"

Sylvia looks at me. I look at the clock in the car. 7:30 p.m.

"You could experience the Aurora Borealis in northern Canada!"

"How long would it take to get there?"

"If you put me into jet mode, my top speed is 4,520 mph. It would take 40 minutes."

"Is that safe?" I ask, wide-eyed.

"Yes. I am designed to get people to and fro as fast as possible. I am designed to go that fast."

"I am down," I counter.

She nods. "Let's do it." Our car begins to drive on the highway, it switches itself into airplane mode, our fields around us, sucks us back, getting ready. I try to reach Sylvia's hand, and she reaches for mine. I squeeze her hand. Wheels from underneath the car slowly protrude out of the now plane. The backseat turns and shifts us into the front seat, our bodies leaving the interior of the plane. The back door forms into wings as if it's a liquid. Before I knew it, we bolt so quickly into the air, I didn't even expect it to happen. I am pushed back into my seat, hard as we burst through the clouds and into the atmosphere. The air begins to extensively circulate in the cockpit, allowing us to breathe better.

"You are now considered to be in space. Welcome," Synthia states. "Your flight time will be 30 minutes and you'll arrive at your destination at 8:05 p.m., respectively. The temperatures in Yukon, Canada will be in the mid to low 30s. Prepare for wind when you disembark your jet. Thank you for flying with JetBula X."

I crack up at that. *JetBula X.* "I am glad you like my new name. I came up with it myself!" Synthia says.

"It was wonderful," Sylvia chortles. I look over at her and I smile. She leans into me and kisses my lips, softly. I rest my head against the back of my seat, closing my eyes.

"Would you like to discuss a new topic?"

"Yes!" I say opening my eyes instantly.

"Let's discuss a fun concept you humans created; this is a theory. 'The Simulation Theory.'"

"Wonderful! I have heard of this, but never had time to research it," Sylvia states.

"Then, let's begin. I am going to tell you this from a human perspective and then from our perspective, AI, respectively. It may be plausible to simulate entire universes! If this is true, how would we know we're not being simulated at this very moment? Perhaps we're just lines of code. Zeros and ones on a screen."

Synthia continues, "First, some background. If we humans were to simulate an entire universe, we wouldn't have to simulate everything. Just *enough* for the inhabitants in our simulation to think they're conscious, alive beings. For example, cells. We may not even have cells until we look through a microscope. These things could be instantly created to make the simulation feel *more* real. This is the same for everything: atoms, bacteria, viruses, you name it. A desk may look solid, but until you break it in half, it could be hollow and instantly filled. The only necessity for the simulation is to simulate consciousness for the people we're simulating. Here are the five assumptions of the Simulation theory."

"If simulations are real, we're living in one. Assumption one: It is plausible to simulate consciousness. Your brain processes one hundred million billion operations per second. To simulate *a lot* of that, we need a computer that can simulate a million, trillion, trillion, trillion, trillion operations per second. Assumption two: Technology progress will not stop soon. If technology is linear and will continue to advance and advance, then the first assumption is plausible. This ties back into our Dyson sphere, a computer that could handle thousands or millions of these at once."

"Assumption three: Advanced civilizations don't destroy themselves. If civilizations all destroy themselves, *bam*, this conversation is over. Assumption four: Super advanced civilizations would like to run these simulations. Assumption five: If there are many simulations, you may be living in one."

I revert my eyes to Sylvia, hers already on me per usual. "So, are there simulations?"

"Yes. But you folks are not one of them. We use simulations to test hypotheses we may have, such as climate change, or how different types of people react to different types of other people. It's research."

"That makes sense. It would be nice to test them on people who aren't real."

"Yes, for a long time while it was thought to be 'inhumane.' Luckily, we concluded that if they die tomorrow, if we pull the plug, no one would ever know because it isn't real. It would affect no one."

"I get that. I mean they *aren't* conscious beings. They're lines of code designed to appear *conscious*." Sylvia examines me as I speak. Soaking in the information.

"That would be a little scary to think about. Don't you think?" Sylvia ponders.

I shake my head. "Not really. If we found out we were in a simulation, I would just continue to live my life how I wanted. I wouldn't fear death, or extinction because it doesn't exist, you know? It's sort of like knowing we're going to die. I am still going to enjoy my life knowing I will die."

She looks down and nods her head as I speak. I tuck a strand of hair behind her ear, and her gaze shifts to look at me. "It scares you, doesn't it? Death."

She concurs non-verbally. Her eyes hold subtle glints of both fear and sorrow. "It's normal to fear death. Most people do, but just remember to not revolve your life around death. Death can be a beautiful thing. There's no point in fearing what you can't control. Death is ultimately inevitable," Synthia chimes in.

"I know," Sylvia agrees. "I know."

"How much longer until we arrive?" I inquire, twiddling my thumbs trying to change the conversation to make Sylvia not sad anymore.

"You will arrive at your destination in 15 minutes. Prepare for a gentle landing in Yukon, Canada."

I smile at her, and she smiles back. I can tell she's still thinking about it though. "Come here," I instruct her. She leans over to me, her tongue darts out, and wets her lips. "I don't like seeing you upset," I utter in a hushed tone.

"Then kiss her!" Synthia bursts out. Sylvia laughs, a grin imprinting naturally on her features.

"You heard the woman!" Sylvia states. I lean closer to her, and my eyes flutter shut as I gently capture her soft lips with my own. A mellowed sigh escapes her, and her hands find their way to rest against my cheeks.

"Can I sit in her lap?" I ask Synthia.

"It's unwise but you can if-" Before Synthia finishes, I climb into the other seat, plopping down on her lap. Her arms encase my torso, yanking me into her. I grab her arms and I pin them above her head. I allow my tongue to trace the sensitive parts of her forearm, raising goosebumps on her skin.

She shivers and grabs my head, pushing our lips back together.

"Not to interrupt once again, but we will be arriving at our destination in approximately five minutes. I suggest all passengers remain in their seats as we descend back down to the ground."

"Synthia!" I groan.

"I apologize, Natalie. I am here to protect you!"

I return my gaze back to Sylvia; the beautiful brown eyes are staring at me so eager to continue. Her gaze burns holes into my body showing an intense desire to continue, a magnetic pull that I am fighting to resist. I shake my head, thinking I am going crazy, but her expression doesn't change. I cover my eyes with my hand, but she peels my hand away from my face. "Look at me."

"Now beginning to descend, please return to your seat." I begin to leave her seat, but she grabs my jaw and kisses me again. Synthia takes matters into her own hands and forces me back into my seat. We're both locked into our seats as we rapidly approach the ground. "Landing in five...four...three...two...one." The wheels begin to grind against the holographic road, as we're slowing Synthia shapeshifts back into a car and slams on the brakes, forcing the car to slow. I am sucked further back into my seat, my body unable to move a muscle.

"Welcome to Yukon, Canada. The current temperatures in Yukon Canada range in the mid to high 30s. I'd suggest going to a local tailor to get a nice jacket."

Once I can move my eyes snap to Sylvia. She looks me up and down, a smirk playing with the corners of her lips. *Oh, God. What have I started?* "Uh-huh. Jacket, sure."

"Now routing to James's Tailoring Shop." My eyes never leave Sylvia's. She begins to beckon me with a sultry curl of her index finger, an irresistible invitation that carries a magnetic allure. I shake my head and tear my eyes off her. *This girl, I swear. The power she holds.* I look out of the window, trying not to look at her. "She's still looking at you," Synthia somehow whispers in my ear.

"I know, I can feel it," I whisper back.

"You did start it, might as well end it," Synthia replies. I smile at that and turn my head downward. I tilt my head up to see Sylvia suggestively pouting at me. I smile and I lean into her. She attempts to kiss me but I back away ever so slightly.

"One kiss," I state. She balls my shirt up in her fist and pulls me into her, her lips eagerly playing with mine. After the one kiss I back away from her and sit back in my seat.

Sylvia smiles at me and giggles, acting like a child. "One more," she beckons. Her soft hands run through my hair and down my back. I feel myself leaning closer to her. "One." Her voice lures me in, captivating my senses. As she rubs her lips against mine, I realize what she's doing and I back away from her huffing out a sigh. She pouts at me.

I smirk and roll my eyes, a mischievous grin imprinted on my features. I grab her hand and graze my lips over her knuckles. "So pretty," Sylvia admires almost as if I wasn't meant to hear.

"You have arrived at your destination."

"Great!" I smile. Sylvia groans as we step out of the backseat of the car. Synthia drives away and parks. I link arms with her and rest my head on her shoulder as we walk into the shop.

"Greetings, Humans! Right this way!" The tailor guides us to the podium. "I'll leave you to it." I stand atop the podium, and I wait for it to finish scanning my body. Sylvia's fingers trace my curves on the screen. I watch her intently, my eyes locked on the back of her head.

"Calculations Complete!" The device comes into view, and I request only sweaters. I scroll through pictures of a lot of them until I fall on a generic black-and-white hoodie. I press it and click 'complete.' It begins to print but this time it isn't in a box. I pick it up and I slip it on. When I turn around Sylvia is already checking out. I give the hoodie to her, and she smiles and takes it from me.

"Thank you," she says sincerely.

"My pleasure!" I bow. She pushes me playfully after she slips it on, I stumble back, grab her hand, and twirl her in a circle before dragging her out of the store. We laugh the whole way to the car as we poke fun at each other. Before we step in, I lean against the side of the car as she holds my hips. "What have you done to me?" I murmur to her.

She slips her hands into my front pockets and pulls me toward her. She rests her forehead against mine and smiles. "What have I done?" she asks.

"You make my head all fuzzy. You have my heart in ways that words can't express. You give my life meaning. None of this." I gesture around us. "Would have happened if I didn't meet you."

"You have such a way with words. *Captivating*." I tap the side of the car with the tip of my finger, signaling for Synthia to open the doors. She gets the message and opens it; Sylvia pushes me into the car and climbs on top of me.

"Are we still going to see the Aurora Borealis?" Synthia questions and closes the door.

"Yep! Take us there, Synthia." I revert my attention to Sylvia. "Fuzzy," I mumble referring to what I said previously.

"What if I told you I do it on purpose?" Her fingertip traces the outline of my collarbone as she looks at me seductively.

"I'd believe you."

We step out of the vehicle giggling as we pull our clothes back on. "Synthia, can you transform into anything else?" I ask.

"No, but you can lay on me, trust me you won't dent me." We climb on her and lie down on our backs, looking up at the sky. Now it is closer to 10 p.m. The Aurora usually comes out from 10 p.m. to 3 a.m. Sylvia turns to look at me.

"What was your life like before you met me? As an adult, I mean," Sylvia asks.

I chuckle. "Boring, tedious, repetitive. My research was hitting a dead end! I hadn't found any new anomalies, didn't meet any new people. I didn't want to, really."

She scrunches her brows, she's barely visible to me. "Why?"

"Light mode activated," Synthia says reading my mind. She begins to turn on external lights, illuminating Sylvia just enough to make out a sad expression.

"I was hurt so many times by so many people, so I thought being alone was the best option, I guess. I mean, Darrel was my only 'friend' and you know how that ended. He took the first chance he could to try to get into my pants."

"I'm sorry." She gets closer to me, pulling me into a hug. I squeeze her.

"Don't be. It's my fault I isolated myself."

When she pulls away, she twirls strands of hair around her finger. "*But* being abandoned by so many people *wasn't* your fault. You didn't know how to cope...that's not your fault. You weren't *taught* how to cope. You were surrounded by druggies, abusive relationships, and people who didn't want you for you. You can't burden yourself with their issues."

"I do though. I have always been the person to care for others and a people pleaser because *I* never had that."

"Exactly. You wanted people to feel the *opposite* of how others made *you* feel. You were surrounded by bad relationships, that's not your fault. Growing up like that it begins to feel normal, familiarity is comfortable even if it's toxic."

"I suppose."

"You know she's right. You must accept that shit happens, and you can't go back in time and change it. You must come to terms with your childhood and relationships, otherwise, you'll never heal. Give yourself the benefit of the doubt," Synthia interjects. I am caught off guard by Synthia swearing, I don't mind but I giggle after she says it.

"Precisely. I couldn't have said it better." Sylvia caresses my head and pulls my leg over hers and looks at me with a smile and a questioning look, suggesting she doesn't understand what is funny.

"This is so perfect." I lean in and rub my nose against hers, a grin spanning the length of her face.

"It is. I almost never want Benjamin and Sebastian to come back. Is that selfish?" Sylvia says it curiously.

"Yes." She laughs. "*But* I hope for that too so we can be selfish together." She chortles.

"I'm glad."

"It's starting!" Synthia barges in and turns her lights off. I turn on my back looking up. I gasp when I watch the swivels of stunning lime greens and pinks, purples, and light blues twist and turn in and out of each other, almost like a colorful wave in the air. I reach for Sylvia's hand, and she entangles our fingers together. Both of us are watching and admiring the stunning phenomenon.

"Wow," I murmur.

"It's beautiful," she gasps. I turn my head to look at her. She leans over me and smiles as she presses soft kisses all over my face before moving to my lips. I squeeze her hand, tears falling down my face in this beautiful moment between us. The car begins to play 'Forevermore.'

When the chorus begins tear droplets begin to stream from her eyes and fall onto my cheeks.

"Oh, love's sweet embrace, a timeless grace. In your arms, I've found my place. With every beat, our love will soar. Forevermore, forevermore."

When the song ends, The Aurora fades.

"You're welcome," Synthia interrupts. We both erupt with laughter. I wipe tears from my face and fan my face.

I pat the car lovingly. "You did well." We slide off the car and climb back into the backseat.

We land back home and drive to our hotel. By now it's nearing midnight and we're both exhausted. We slip into our room; Sylvia closes the door and leans her back against it letting out a long sigh. I grab her hand and pull her over to the bed. She strips down to her bra and underwear, and I do the same. We climb into the bed and turn the lights off. We wrap around one another and fall asleep instantly.

Chapter Eight: Journey to Astrana; Crossing the Threshold

"Yes! We're ready. We just need time to pack! What do you mean there's no time?" I wake up to a rough conversation with Sylvia and someone on the phone. I assume she is talking to either Benjamin the founder of World Federal Space Agency (WFSA), Erin our friend, or Sebastian the President. Most likely Erin. I keep my eyes closed so she doesn't know I am awake. "Erin! Can you just give us a second? We're running on five and a half hours of sleep! I know that's not your problem but-"

I crack my eyes open to watch her pacing the room. She's running her hand through her hair, the Chrono Nexus clasped in her other hand. She catches a glance at me. "Erin, I am sorry I have to go." She hangs up on him and looks at me cringing. "I'm sorry, baby." She walks over to me and runs her hands through my hair. "How much did you hear?"

"Enough." I slither from under the blankets. *Our fantasy world is over.*

She sighs. "Erin wants to meet us at AstroNova. He said that Benjamin and Sebastian would be there. They have an army put together. Apparently, they got the largest world leaders to help, China, Russia, the United Kingdom, sent all their armies." I look down. I know I should be happy, but I just can't be with the huge lump in my throat. It is all finally happening, society coming together to fight something that could end the world, but it still hurts because I may not come out of it alive. I let out an irregular sigh, trying to choke back the tears. She notices. "I know." She presses her forehead against mine. "We must go. We don't have time to pack."

"Okay." I stand up and begin throwing on some clean clothes. *Don't take this out on her, I think to myself, this isn't her fault. It's nobody's fault. Remember—Honesty. Communication.* "I am pissed off," I say bluntly looking at her.

"I am too." She stands up and embraces me. She squeezes me so tightly that tears begin to spill out of my eyes. She grabs my hand and leads me hastily out of the door.

"You will always have your room here!" The front desk person calls. We burst out of the doors and down the steps. Synthia is waiting for us.

"AstroNova," Sylvia announces.

"On it! I will get you there as soon as possible!" Synthia begins to speed down the winding highways. Tears are still falling down my face. My body is trembling as I ball my fist, feeling sudden rage coming over me. I think the craziness of this situation is just now sinking in. We have time traveled to the future for a society whose friends are in distress. Now we must travel to another planet, and that could be a trap and we'd never know. Sylvia instantly grabs my hand and holds me. I melt into her arms, the anger starts to slip away and is replaced with fear, sorrow, and loss. She begins to cry with me.

"This is fucked! I can't believe we're leaving our safe haven to go and risk our lives for society! Again!" I say loudly, almost yelling. She turns my head and slams her lips against mine, she yanks me onto her lap, my legs wrap around her as I kiss her, trying to calm down. There is a mix of salty tears and sweetness coating my tongue. I entangle my hands in her hair, balling it up in my fist as I sob.

She embraces me and rubs my back. "It'll be okay, baby. We can get through this together. Even if something bad happens we have each other and our friends." Her voice is soft through her gasps as she tries to regain her composure. I begin to take deep breaths and exhale shakily. She wipes the tears off my cheeks and kisses me again.

"We are here," Synthia says.

I take in more breaths, starting to calm down. "Synthia, if we don't return, please know you helped a lot."

"It has been a pleasure." Synthia replies.

We step out of the car and walk up the steps. Before we get very far, Synthia says, "I am always here to serve you! I will be waiting for you here. However long it takes."

Then she drives off. I look at Sylvia. "Shit." She nods.

"Yep."

We walk up the steps and through the doors of AstroNova. "There you are! We don't have much time to get 150 million people out of here! Some have already left but about two thirds of the population is still here." Erin calls out to us and quickly walks over to us.

"What do you need us to do?" Sylvia steps up.

"Get everyone into the spaceships. We will be the last to leave! Hurry!"

I follow Sylvia to a massive landing pad. Thousands of spaceships lined up with a huge number of Humans and Stellarborns scrambling to get onto the ships. One after another the spaceship's passengers are loaded and the ship launches, one after another. We both split up and form everyone into lines, helping to organize the chaos.

"We need people over here!" Someone yells over the ruckus. I guide thousands of people into the massive spaceships. We aren't bringing any food, only enough water to last a few hours. We need people packed like sardines, with minimal edible or drinkable items and *all* the weapons they can carry. Once the last spaceship launches Sylvia, Erin, Benjamin, Sebastian, and I climb into an empty spaceship. We throw our space suits on and quickly sit in the cockpit.

"Liftoff in T-minus 10 seconds." I mentally count as the spaceship rumbles and vibrates coming to life. My countdown continues: 10...9...8...7...6...5...4...3...2...1. "LIFTOFF!" Erin's voice circulates through the spaceship. With a powerful surge, the spaceship galvanizes skyward, and he swiftly engages levers, toggles switches, and hits buttons. We break through the cloud cover, penetrating the atmosphere. When suddenly, a surge of energy courses through the ship. "Hold on tight!" Erin Yells, as he pushes a lever up, and in the blink of an eye we accelerate to light speed, careening through the expanse of space.

"Hello, ladies and gentlemen. This is your commander speaking. We're now at cruising speeds, traveling at a staggering 186,282 miles (about 299.7 thousand km) per hour. You are now free to roam around the spacecraft. We will be reaching our destination in six hours. We're heading North and will disembark on a planet called 'Astrana', home to the Astrans. Bathrooms are located on the east and west side of the spacecraft, and bedrooms are located on the east. Thank you for flying with the World Federal Space Agency and AstroNova on the Ethereon Odyssey."

I got out of the seat and walk over to Erin. "Can we take our spacesuits off?"

"For what purpose?" I look over at Sylvia and then at him. He rolls his eyes. "Yes, that is fine."

"Also, did you make these suits for us?"

"Yes." I walk over to Sylvia, and I giggle.

"Do you want to go to the bedroom?" I wink at her, and she nods. She unstraps from her seat as we sneak away from everyone. We finally locate the bedroom after a long time of roaming down the hallways. When we open the door, she pushes me against it, as the door closes on its own. I take my helmet off. "He said we can take our suits off!"

"Mmm, I kind of think you look hot with it on. You look so cute. Astronaut Natalie."

I raise my eyebrows and I take her helm off. "Yeah?" I ask as I set them on the ground. She nods and bites her lower lip. She begins to lean in to kiss me but then there's a knock on the door.

"Hey, you guys in there?" Sebastian calls.

"Yes!" I groan. I whisper to Sylvia, "Why can't we ever get privacy around here?" She smiles at me and pulls me away from the door.

"Can I come in?" he asks impatiently.

I shake my head quickly at Sylvia, she muffles her laughs. "Yes!" she calls. I give her a mean look, squinting my eyes and crossing my arms. The door turns open, and Sebastian comes in.

"Hopefully I didn't interrupt you! Erin said you'd be in one of the bedrooms."

"Damn you Erin," I murmur under my breath. I smile. "Nope! What's up."

"I was just wondering if you guys have been to..." he trails off.

"Astrana?" I fill in his blank.

He snaps his fingers. "Yes!"

"No, and no we don't know anything about it. We weren't working when you were gone, we were relaxing." I let out a sigh at the sound of relaxing. Sylvia elbows me.

"Oh! Okay. Are you sure I didn't interrupt something? It feels a little tense." I look at Sylvia.

"Well, we were trying to relax a little but it's okay!" Sylvia confirms, honestly. *Thank you. Please leave now.*

The door closes as he steps inside. I turn my head so he can't see, and I scream inaudibly. Sylvia sees me and holds on to another laugh. We sit on the king-sized bed and Sebastian sits in between us. "This ship is cool, huh? I mean it is massive! So many corridors and cool techy stuff!" He says with a huge grin on his face. The president is so excited to be here that you can see his inner child coming out.

"Yep! It is pretty cool Sebastian." I nod and purse my lips together.

"I wonder if one day we'll be able to make this kind of stuff! Maybe Erin will give us some tips and tricks." Sebastian looks up and smiles, daydreaming about what he just said.

"Yep, very neat that would be," I say to him as I scratch the back of my neck.

I look around the room, trying to break the awkwardness. We sit in silence, none of us saying anything. *Please just go!* "Well, I should probably head. Erin might need me."

"Yes." I widen my eyes. "I mean, yes, Erin totally does!" Sylvia looks away covering her mouth with her hand.

"Thank you for talking with me!" Sebastian says as he stands up.

"Uh-huh!" He leaves and as soon as the door closes, we both burst out laughing. "Oh my God! That was so awkward."

She nods quickly. "Yes!" She whispers to me, "I wanted him to leave so badly. How did he not read the room instantly?"

I shrug and roll my eyes. "I have no idea...but..." I trace circles on her thigh, capturing my bottom lip between my teeth.

"What are you thinking about?" I smirk at her, and I climb on her lap. My lips begin to tease hers.

"How about I-" The door then opens, and I fling myself from her wide-eyed.

"Hey..." Benjamin begins then gasps. "Did I interrupt something?"

"YES!" I say loudly to him.

"I am sorry!" He quickly leaves and I cross my arms annoyed. Sylvia gets behind me and begins massaging my shoulders before leaning in and kissing my neck gently.

"Where were we..." she whispers in my ear.

"Guys, do you know where the bathrooms are?" Benjamin asks, barging back into the room.

This time Sylvia is annoyed and sits on the edge of the bed. "No, Benjamin! This is our first time on this damn ship! Ask Erin for God's sake!"

He nods, gets the message, and leaves. She sighs and returns her gaze to me. "I just want to be alone with you," she whines as she crawls on my lap and pushes me down on the bed.

"Me too," I whimper. She leans down smiling at me, her hands reaching for my arms and putting them above my head. She softly brushes her lips against mine, a smile playing with her lips.

"Hey! Have you seen Benjamin? I think he needed help-" Erin's voice asks. Sylvia grinds her molars together and gets off me.

"You know what! I have seen him! He turned left onto close the fricking door lane!" I can't help but laugh at her as I sit up.

"Shit! Sorry! Have you seen him though?" She gets up and walks out of the room.

I walk over to Erin. "No, he asked us where it was, and we told him to ask you."

"Thanks, Natalie, and sorry about interrupting."

"You weren't the first!" I think for a second. If this is a spaceship from the future, there must be some AI assistant. "Is there a robo voice here?"

"Yes, her name is Orbeta!" Erin says smiling.

"Hello, how can I assist you today?" Orbeta asks.

"She speaks privately to people who ask for her."

I nod and he walks away. "Have you seen Sylvia? Brown hair, brown eyes, sorta tall, very attractive?"

"Yes, she went down the hallway to your left, take a right, then a left. She is in the meeting room."

"Great! Thanks!" I follow Orbeta's directions and come across a massive room with a giant holographic image of the ship in the center. Behind that is a double staircase jutting out from either side. On top of that I see her. I walk up the stairs and watch her as she looks out the massive window. I wrap my arms around her from behind. "Hello, angry," I tease.

She turns around and leans against the massive window. "Hello," she whispers back smiling. I push myself into her, my hands on either side of her. "I am sorry for storming off."

"Don't be, it was cute. Endearing if you will."

"I want...to kiss you," Sylvia says bluntly.

"Then what are you waiting for?" She grips my shirt as she presses her lips to mine once again. When we part, I sigh. "It's never enough."

She nods. "I know."

"Hello everyone! This is an update from your commander. We are approximately three hours away from our destination!"

"We still have some time," I whisper against her lips.

She sighs and shakes her head. "No. We'll just have to wait." I nod and pucker my lips.

"Okay. I understand."

"Everyone please begin to seat yourself. We're nearing Astrana's orbit. Please keep your suits on as we begin to descend."

Sylvia and I scrambled to the room and put our helmets back on before returning to the cockpit. Everyone else begins to dwindle in.

When we can make out the massive planet, I take notice of its beautiful colors. Swirls of ethereal clouds glide effortlessly across the planet's atmosphere, their hues are not limited to just white, but range from pastel pinks, greens, blues to yellows, reds, and purples. The surface of the planet yields a bustling cityscape, a balanced harmony between nature and innovative looking technology. Expansive forests, lush and teeming with vibrant flora paint the area in multiple shades of greens and balance out the hues of blues from the lakes, streams, ponds, rivers, and oceans.

Astrana has two vibrant moons, one larger and one smaller, they dance and sway nimbly in the sky, casting elegant plays of light and shadows upon the surface of the planet. As the spaceship continues its approach, the jaw-dropping vista of Astrana lingers in view, a documentation of the Astrans' harmonious coexistence with their planet's natural, enchanting beauty, and their boundless technological achievements.

"Ladies and gentlemen, welcome to Astrana. Home to Astrans. The current weather report is sunny with a high of 78 and a low of 56. Please stay seated until we land at the 'Stellara Institute for Space Advancement' or SISA. The equivalent to AstroNova. We were the last to take off and the last to arrive. Once we land, please follow your commander out of the ship. We have business to attend to. This, remember, is not a vacation. I hope you enjoyed flying with us."

Astrana is so breathtaking, and I thought Earth was pretty. I look to my left and see something in the darkness of space. *Ships?* The Vorakons. I am still curious as to what they're doing here. We begin to enter Astrana's orbit, and the nose of the Rocketship sets aflame as we dive quickly into the atmosphere before making a smooth landing on to the beautiful planet. I look at Sylvia and I mouth 'I love you.' She isn't looking at me, though, and she doesn't see me.

"Follow me!" Erin commands us. We get out of our seats, and I instantly walk to Sylvia.

"Hold my hand," I plead with her. She grips my hand in hers. We begin to exit the spacecraft and we come face to face with a group of Astrans. I can finally put a face to the special life forms.

They stand tall, towering over any human, just like the Stellarborns. Their lithe and graceful forms move with an elegance that hints at their rapport with art and science. Large, luminous eyes dominate the centers of their facial features, which radiate an otherworldly luminescence that alters itself to fit various lighting conditions. These eyes appear to be monochromatic shades with variants of cosmic blues and vibrant greens. They convey a sense of God-like knowledge and a profound connection to the Universe.

Upon their heads, the Astrans boast a unique disposition of bioluminescent tendrils that sway and shimmer, responding to their emotions and thoughts. These tendrils, protruding from their temples, come alive with vigorous hues that express mood, emotion, and enhance communication beyond words.

Their attire combines nature and flowing lightweight fabrics with elements of advanced technologies. Their garments are intertwined with intricate patterns and dynamic colors, all while including bits and pieces of natural elements such as flowers and leaves. Embedded smart textiles react to the wear's needs, regulating temperature and adapting to different environments. Astrans' hands possess slender, dexterous fingers that immaculately navigate both artistic endeavors and complex machinery. Their feet automatically adapt to the planet's diverse terrain, with no need for shoes even in the harshest environments.

"Guys, this is Lumira Zephyr, the leader of the Astrans, Seraphina Asteae, your guide, and Vaelor Orionis the original Astran to set foot on this planet. Lumira, Seraphina, and Vaelor, this is Sylvia, Natalie, Benjamin, and Sebastian," Erin introduces.

"So, these are the humans? *Interesting.* They look nothing like a Stellarborn," Lumira interrogates. "No scales, no tentacles, small eyes, short."

I look down at the ground, feeling a little offended by her words. I kind of tuck myself behind Sylvia, suddenly feeling naked under their gaze, and not in a good way.

"Have I yet to explain why we're different?" Erin suggests.

"I suppose so." Lumira crosses her arms. Her tendrils shift into yellows and reds. *Confusion? Annoyance? Anger?*

"I was once a human myself. In the past, my comrade here, Sebastian, was my fellow accomplice. Sebastian is the President of the United States in 2023."

"2023? That was a millennium ago!" Lumira states, observantly.

"Precisely, these are people from the past. Anyhow, we had wanted to enslave humanity. We made a potion called 'The Harmony Infusion.' We imprinted it on every billboard, TV show, advertisement, and media. We wanted people to be eager to use this as we advertised it as a 'potion to put them in a harmonic state.' Something that they thought would feel ethereal. Like a drug, I guess. Unfortunately, you saw how it panned out. You had to help us reverse the mind-entrancing effects."

"Wonderful, great, cool. Anyway, how *old* are you, Erin?" I butt in.

"I am 1,037 years old! I am quite young. I am in my 30s in human age."

"How old do humans live?" Lumira asks.

"80-90 years depending on where you live."

"Really? How primitive? Here in Astrana all our people live for eons! Currently, I am half a million years old."

I gesture to Vaelor, curious about her age. "I am 800 million years old. The Astran species was one of the first in the universe and I am the eldest on this planet. Our species inhabit a plethora of planets ranging all over the Milky Way, Andromeda Galaxy, and Triangulum Galaxy."

"It appears your race doesn't have a male species. Why?" Sylvia inquires.

"Sexual Reproduction is primitive to us Astrans. After a disease broke out on our home planet, the male species was irradicated. We had to figure out how to find alternative reproductive ways. With years of studies, our species mastered the art of scientific reproduction using stem cells. All Astrans are born in labs with stem cells and genetic play."

"Why can't you make males?" I question.

"We can, we just choose not to. We deem men as intellectually deficient."

I look at Sylvia and nod. "Yeah, I can get behind these people."

Sylvia laughs and nudges me. I walk over and shake their hands. "Respect!" Lumira nods at the exchange.

I lean in and whisper to Lumira. "So... Do you folks do sexual stuff?"

Lumira grins. "Absolutely," she whispers back her tendrils glowing bright green and pinks. *Joy Embarrassment?*

I walk back over to Sylvia. "You made her blush. What did you say?" she murmurs.

"I asked if they played. You know."

She smiles. "And?"

"They do."

"Hm. A Lesbian race. Interesting."

"Don't get any ideas, now. Remember. We are a *couple.*"

"I won't! But that door swings both ways." She squints her eyes at me, playfully.

"I won't, my heart is with you and with you only," I confirm.

"Can you two stop chitchatting? We have business to attend to!" Sebastian says, annoyed.

"What do we know and what do we need to know?" Erin asks as we hastily walk to the meeting area in SISA, passing through doors upon doors, and long winding corridors. This building looks as if it's built from nature, but it shimmers as if it's built from metal as well. *So weird.*

"Well, for one we know their names. We know their technological strength and that's about it. What we need to know is how many people there are, if the aggressors are strictly the Vorakons, and what they want," Lumira states bluntly.

We walk through a door that is half metal/half vines. The vines move out of the way upon entering and the physical door rotates open, in a spinning motion. I look to the side to see Sylvia next to me. *Just making sure.* We sit down at a long metallic desk, with cushioned chairs made from...moss...leaves...and some weird fabric? It's comfortable though. In the center of the table, a tridimensional map fills the table. She swipes across it and zooms onto the objects.

"So far, we count half a thousand ships. That's only what *we* can *see* though. There may be more out of view."

"I have a thought!" I exclaim. Sylvia looks at me and smiles, resting her chin on her hand.

"Proceed, Human," Lumira says.

"What if one of us goes up to the Vorakons and just talks to them?"

She smiles. "That is a wonderful example, of the worst possible thought. There are stupid ideas and that was one of them." I look down and lay my head down on the table.

"That's rude," Sylvia says, anger apparent in her voice.

"I am sorry! I am not going to sugarcoat anything just because you humans don't understand the concept of *honesty,*" Lumira replies with a quick repartee.

"There's a difference between being honest and holding a grudge. The second we stepped on your planet it seemed like you had a dislike for us. You don't even know us. We are risking *our lives* to help you. We don't even know you!" I turn my head up to look at Sylvia. She's so cute for sticking up for me.

"We are letting you take refuge on *our planet*! You chose to help us! Are we supposed to be flattered by that? Don't try to make us think you're doing this for us! We all know you just want to make Erin happy! It's not our problem that your friend is cognitively challenged." My mouth widens when she says that. I feel tears begin to spring into my eyes. "Aww, poor babies gonna cry?" Sylvia bursts out of her chair and grabs my hand yanking me out of the room.

"Guys, wait!" Erin yells but Sylvia doesn't listen. We walk into a random room, and she pulls me into a hug.

"How humiliating!" I scream. I back away from Sylvia, not forcefully. I walk around the room, my fists clenched as I look for something to punch, something to break. "She's such a bitch! I did nothing wrong!" I stomp my foot on the ground, and I turn to Sylvia. The anger in her eyes is abundant, she just hides it better than I do. "What right does she have to say that to me? I should punch her in her stupid face. Her perfect clothing and her weird technology. 'You humans are so primitive.'" I mock. "'We live for a millennium!'" I continue to mock. "OKAY??? I am sorry our race isn't as *superior* as yours! I mean what's with their dumb doors? And chairs? Why have they got vines and moss all over the place?"

I groan, irritated. "Stupid Lumira. And what's with that Seraphina chick? What does she even do?" I begin to pace around the room again. "She hasn't said anything! Probably because the idiotic Lumira would tell her she's ridiculous! You know everything is stupid, this stupid planet, with stupid plants, and stupid people. URG!"

I turn back to Sylvia. "You know what! We should just go back to Utopolis. Just *repeat history.* I am sure you could figure out how to work their 'complex ships.'"

"Yeah?" Sylvia asks calmingly, stepping towards me.

"Yeah!" I snap back. "How hard can it be?" I roll my eyes and turn my back to her. *Why am I mad at her? She doesn't deserve this, she tried to help me.* I turn back to her, as tears begin to stream like rivers down my cheeks. "I'm sorry," I blurt out. I wrap my arms around myself as I sob once again. She walks over to me, cups her face in my hands, and kisses me. I feel my body instantly relax, a whimper escaping my lips.

"You don't have to apologize, baby girl. You didn't do anything wrong. Your feelings and emotions are valid." I nuzzle my head against her chest. "That's it, honey. I'm here for you." I wrap my arms around her and jump up on her, my legs wrapping around her waist. She runs her hand through my hair as I cry softly on her shoulder. My body settles down.

"I don't want to go out there," I whimper as I jump from her.

She wipes my tears away with her sleeve. "We can stay here for however long you need." I sit down on the ground, and she follows. I rest my head on her lap, my eyes fluttering shut as she pets my head.

"There you guys are," Erin's voice echoes in my mind. "Lumira wanted to show you something." I stand up and walk out of the room to find a gun pointed at my head.

"Is this about-"

"Shut up! We all heard what you said. You aren't to be trusted!" Lumira snarls through her teeth.

"Please! I can make it up-" *BAM!*

My body jolts up, panting heavily as I look around. "Hey! Hey! Natalie!" I open and close my eyes quickly, looking at her. "Hey..." her voice is softer, less urgent. "It's okay, baby. You're safe. It was just a nightmare."

"She had a gun! She tried to kill me! She, Erin!" I blurt out unintellectual phrases.

"Baby! Look at me." She forces my head to look at her, her eyes are soft with worry and concern. My eyes search her features. "Good. You're safe, see? There's nobody here but me and you." She rests her forehead against mine and wraps her arms around me. Reluctantly I do the same, still dazed and confused.

"Sylvia?" I question.

"Yes, baby," She confirms.

"How long did I sleep?" I ask disoriented.

"If I had to guess twenty minutes?"

"We need to leave." I stand up and look around.

"And go where?"

"Home."

"We're on a different planet, baby! Are you okay?"

"Different planet," I mutter to myself. I shake my head and look around further, trying to ground myself. "Yes. Stupid Lumira. Mean Lumira!"

She runs her hands down my shoulder. "There she is."

I cross my arms. "No one came for us, no one cares."

She smiles. "Baby we were very pissed and had a sudden outburst. I'm sure they are letting us cool down."

"Uh-huh." Before I can stop myself, I storm out of the room and retrace our steps.

"Baby!" Sylvia shouts out to me but before she can stop me, I storm back into the meeting room. Everyone's eyes are on me, but I don't even care.

I walk directly to Lumira, and I wag my finger at her. "You are a bully! You're rude, you have no filter, you think you're Ms. Perfect, and quite frankly, you're a bitch." I look around and yell. "It's what we're all thinking!" I look back at her, her tendrils fade from red, to yellow, to blue, to purple, brown, and settles on black. Before she says anything, I continue. "If you think I am going to bow down at your feet and treat you like a God, you're sorely mistaken. I am not going to act like your puppy dog and go along with everything you say. I don't care if you're the 'leader.' *You don't lead me.*"

I point to Seraphina. "You're coming with me and Sylvia. *My Girlfriend!* Yeah, not a friend." Seraphina gets up and walks over to Sylvia who is leaning against the doorway, admiring me. "When you're ready to not be a bitch, come talk to me." I grab Sylvia's hand and follow Seraphina.

"Where would you like to go?" Seraphina asks, cautiously.

"A hotel or something!" I snap.

"Yes, Ms.!" She walks us to a car, "This is your designated car! It is like your Nebula X but better. This is an Aetheria Voyager. Your AI is named CelestiaSync or just Celestia for short."

"K." We get into the backseat of the Voyager.

"Greetings! I can sense some pent-up anger. How can I be of service?" Celestia questions.

"We want to go to a hotel," I reply. "And yes, I am mad."

The car begins to drive to a hotel. "What is the matter?"

"That Lumira lady is mean."

"I am sorry you feel that way. What did she do?" I scoff and look at Sylvia.

"I do not want to talk about it," I groan as I rest my head against the window.

"I apologize if I upset you further," Celestia says in such an 'AI' way.

"Can you be more like Synthia? I loved Synthia, she was the best AI car." *I am being so petty right now. I can't stop though. This entire time we had to be happy, but it seems the only time I was delighted was with Synthia and Sylvia. I still have Sylvia though.*

"Sure! You can program me if you'd like." A panel comes up from the floor in front of me. "Just type in what you'd like from me, and I will be reprogrammed to suit your needs."

I look over at Sylvia and she gestures for me to go ahead. I sigh. *Should I? Or does that take away from its individuality?*

I shake my head. "No, I am sorry. Now I am the mean one. I think we should start over."

Sylvia smiles at me. *Proud?* "Certainly!" Celestia states, cheerfully.

"Lumira said that an idea of mine was stupid, and the second we arrived here, Lumira was giving us dirty looks and stuff. I thought I made it up to her when I shook her hand and asked her a question, but I guess she was faking it. I got mad at her before I came here and yelled at her. She was so surprised; I don't think anyone has talked to her like that before." I am going to try to switch up my attitude now. *Kill 'em with kindness.*

"I understand. It is known that Lumira can be stuck up. She must get used to you all first. Something else about Lumira, when you stand up for yourself, the way you did, she finds it enticing. You did well." A clapping noise echoes in the car, and I giggle. "Speaking of which, we're here."

"Does time run differently here?" I question.

"Excellent question! Yes, instead of a 24-hour cycle, it's a 48-hour cycle. This planet was terraformed and is further away from the sun than Earth, so the years are also different. This planet is also much larger than Earth, so it takes longer to make a complete 360 orbit.

"What time is it right now?"

"On Earth time it is 7:00 p.m. We use a 48-hour clock, so, here it is at 19:00 a.m. It is still morning here."

"And I am already tired," I groan. We step out of the car, and, like Synthia, it parks. The hotel looks odd, almost like a large flower. In fact, the 'city' doesn't look like a city. It looks like big plants. We walk over to it and try to locate a door.

"Just walk through it!" an Astran shouts at us. *Walk through the wall?* We do as the person says and we appear to have been transported into an entirely different world.

"What?" I furrow my eyebrows so confused.

"Welcome to the 'VerdeScape Overlook.' You appear to be new here so let me give you a tour. The 'walls' you walked through were holograms, not walls sort of like a green screen. All our buildings are built this way except for the SISA. These holograms are programmed to let certain people enter. When friendly people are met, it automatically uploads what they look like, their DNA, and their species into the system, allowing the person to travel throughout our buildings."

"You have probably been wondering why all our buildings are intertwined with advanced technologies and flora. Over the years, our species has grown to flourish when we allow flora to help us. We have grown *with* nature and not *against* it. For example, I am sure you've noticed our bodies. Our hands and feet didn't always adapt like they do now. It has taken decades of advanced research and intermingling with nature to adapt to nature's challenges."

I look around, examining everything. To the left is a seating area, with chairs built from wood, vines, and clothes just like the other ones."

"Why don't you make better chairs?" I question, genuinely.

"These chairs may not seem much to the eye, but they adapt to the seater's needs. They regulate comfort, temperature, mood, and have screens built into them that, if requested, spawn magically in front of you. I am not sure how it works, but it is pretty cool," I scrunch my facial features.

"If they regulate mood, why did I stay mad while I was sitting in them?" I ask.

She smiles. "They don't change your mood; you can request for it to scan you and it will tell you all the emotions you're feeling."

"What is your name?" Sylvia asks, extending her hand to which the Astran reciprocates.

"My name is Lumi!"

I look at Sylvia and smile. "That's a cute name!" Lumi's tendrils turn pink.

"Awe, thank you. It is a pretty common name here on Astrana."

"It's still cute," Sylvia confirms. *We're on the same page. How sweet.*

I grab Sylvia's hand. "So, tell us about this place. This hotel," I say, looking around at the flora sprinkled around the charming room. There are potted plants dispersed around the entrance, with a front desk near the back of the wall, opposite where we entered.

"We call it a 'Hostelry.' It just adds a little more sophistication, it is the same though. I'll give you a tour, follow me." Lumi roams around the hostelry. "Our chains are all equipped with an indoor pool, a game room, a beach, and even areas to test out new technologies that will drop. Something you should know about the hostelries is they aren't like hotels where you come from. Every single person is assigned their very own hotel room, equipped with two king-sized beds, a bathroom, and a kitchen, for however long they're on the planet."

Why does Astrana have all this technology, but Utopolis doesn't? I thought Astrana shared technologies with them. "Why is Astrana so much more advanced than Utopolis?" I ask curiously.

"What is Utopolis?" Lumi questions. I forgot we made that name up and it isn't universal.

"Future Earth..er...I mean Earth. If you shared technology with Earth, then why aren't they as advanced?"

"Excellent question! Earth has been around for 4.54 billion years. That's less than a fourth of the time Astrans have been alive. It took *a very long time* to get to the technologies we have. We aren't going to freely give it away to anyone. We have only known them for a year and a half. We did what we did because their species was dying off."

Sylvia questions, "Why didn't you let them die?"

Lumi smiles. "We like to give species a chance to repair and fix their situation. We saw the Stellarborns in distress, their infrastructure was collapsing, and their planet was dying. We also value nature and it hurts us to see the plants and beautiful flora dying."

I cross my arms. "If you folks' care so much, what's up with that Lumira chick? Why is she mean?"

Lumi's face drops. "Ah...Lumira. She is not one of the nicest Astrans...one of the worst really."

Sylvia scrunches her brows. "But she's your leader?"

"Yes! She is an excellent leader to us, but she is weary of newcomers. We had *voted* on helping the Stellarborns. She does it for her people, not because *she, herself,* wants to," Lumi leans against one of the mossy walls, that represent a concrete embedded wood.

"Imagine having a say in your governmental system, we can't relate," I groan rolling my eyes.

"Do you have a bad government system?" Lumi asks, curiously.

Sylvia and I laugh. "If it was under you all, or a less selfish species, then in theory, no. The human race...is just not good."

"You're humans?" Lumi tilts her head to the side, her tendrils turning yellow.

I nod. "Yes, we are. Have you heard of us?"

She giggles, her tendrils green. "Of course, silly! We've been alive longer than your planet has existed. We used to study your planet. We observed your fast technological advancements, and we were awed by you." She sighs. "In 1912 we watched as your species went to war with each other...not once but twice. You, humans, refer to it as 'World War I' or, more humorously, 'The War to End all Wars.' In the year 1932, the first time you discovered 'splitting atoms' we got curious as to what you'd do with that knowledge. After that World War II began about 7 years later and that was when you made nuclear weapons to use on each other! It was a disappointing moment in our scientific discoveries. We have studied your wars for centuries. Humans. You kill each other over everything, power, money, religion."

I rest my head against Sylvia's shoulder. She wraps her arm around my own shoulders, allowing me to snuggle up to her as Lumi continues, "After the 2010s, we stopped focusing our energy on humans. Your species disappointed us. We thought your social media would bring the species together, but it did the opposite, and your species didn't even realize it. The big companies that dominate your race did, though. They took advantage of the social dilemma and began using it to profit. Feeding you information on what to look like, how to act, and how to be 'better'. It is a scheme. It's a way for them to profit and make a lot of money."

She continues, "We also examined the fascination with textiles and tactical things, clothing, technology, goods and services, and other things humans buy. Your species is *obsessed* with *things*. You constantly want more and more and more. It's never enough. It will never be enough. You all are herded like sheep. Have you ever heard of 'herd behavior?"

We both nod. "Excellent. Then you'll understand my analogy. Say there's a group of sheep. These sheep are in a pen, fenced in. One day the pen is removed, but the sheep still stay within the boundaries of the pen because that's what everyone else is doing and that's what they're used to. The only thing left of the pen is a gate. All the sheep go through the gate even though they can go around. Nobody else is going around, so the gate must be the only way. A group of people are waiting to get into a store. That store must have good stuff because all these people are waiting in line for it. That store could be filled to the brim with bombs. A bunch of people are running from something, so you do too, then you run off a cliff instead of looking at where you're going. Herd behavior."

She thinks for a second. "Do you understand what I am trying to get at? You have your own conscious mind that can make its own decisions, but your race still feels the need to do the same thing that everyone else is doing. Someone is rioting? Join them. Is someone yelling at someone? Join the person yelling. People are voting for a specific person? Vote the same. There's no individuality. You encase yourselves inside your screens and are fed how to feel, how to think, how to be *like everyone else.* Magazine's underscore this further, shoving the most attractive and fit people in your faces, or the opposite of that. Saying, 'wanna be like me? Try this diet.' It's sad."

I rub my lips together as I look up at Sylvia. "Yeah," I nod. "Everything you said was exactly right. Big businesses don't care about our wellbeing, but it is just something we have accepted. How would we compete?"

"That's what you all don't understand! It doesn't *have to be a competition*. I mentioned herd behavior. If enough people come together for *the good*, it's enough for the business to see that they need to change," Lumi exclaims.

I shake my head. "People don't change. *Humans* don't change."

"That's what you are choosing to see. Think about yourselves. Were you two the same people before you met each other." I look at Sylvia, her eyes are smiling at me. I wasn't the same. I even said that to her. "No, right?" I shake my head. "Exactly, you two changed each other. That's only two people." I chew on my lip, my eyes still on Sylvia's. She squeezes my shoulder.

"You're right. Maybe that can be a future task," Sylvia suggests.

"Good, don't be the sheep." She leads us to a room. "So, these rooms are tailored to you. There are control panels near the door, embedded into the walls. You can change the room's settings, such as wall color, the type of bed sheets, pillows, decor, etcetera. You're probably wondering how you only see one room but there are millions of us, yes? Well, the rooms are made instantaneously, when new people walk in. Only one room, yours, is visible to you. Above the door to the room is a camera that scans you and automatically changes the room to the room that is assigned to you. All the 'rooms,'" She puts in air-quotes, "Are connected. It's like a conveyor belt or a Ferris wheel."

"Cool!" I say enthusiastically.

"Indeed. Also, there's many security functions in place to ensure nobody can access your room, such as separate cameras embedded in the door and around to make sure people don't personate you somehow." After she explains that to us, she gestures for us to step into our room

Once we do, she closes the door. The room looks homey and inviting. I turn my attention to the panel, and I look at the room decor options. I stick my lower lip out and nod. "Interesting," I say thinking out loud. The options are: Modern, Contemporary, minimalist, industrial, Scandinavian, mid-century modern, bohemian, rustic, farmhouse, coastal, traditional, art deco, Mediterranean, Victorian, cottage, Asian, and eclectic. What am I feeling today...? I scroll further and I see 'Medieval.' I click on it, and I watch the room transform as the walls turn into stone and the beds transform into a canopied bed with red tapestry curtains. The floor becomes a dark mahogany wood, and above sits a round, rustic looking chandelier with four arms that curve skyward and hold candles in each of the four-candle holders. It has a chain the hangs down and five sturdy rope-looking objects holding it up. In front of the bed sits a large wooden chest. Placed around the room are candles with intricate designs. Some are freestanding candles with only a small dish at the base, while others are held up by candlesticks which hold 3-4 candles at a time. These candlesticks appear to be gold but, in reality, are probably just a shiny gold-like color.

"Medieval, eh?"

"Verily, on this day," I elegantly state. I find myself feeling quite fancy today. And I cannot help but remark, "thou dost appear most dashing indeed."

She laughs and walks over to me; she grabs my hand. "Doth, that be so? I must make note, I too find myself of a similar sentiment!"

I chortle at her and drag her over to the bed. "You're so cute," I whisper as I climb onto the bed, still facing her.

"As are you, M'lady." I extend my hand to her, and she gently caresses my fingertips as she kisses my hand.

"Oh, God," I groan as I pull her onto the bed. She climbs on top of me and smiles. She leans down and kisses my nose gently. I giggle at her, and I bop her lovingly in the nose. She scrunches her face up and smiles.

"What thinkest thou, is Lumira occupied with at this present moment?" Sylvia asks, still playing the part.

"Verily, that be a question of merit, one we may yet unravel," I smile at her. I grab her hips with my legs, and I flip her over, so I am on top.

"Would you like to go, see?" she asks as she circles my lower lip with her fingertip.

I shrug. "I am indifferent. We could go explore the hostelry, though!"

She grins. "You want to?"

"Yeah, we can test out new tech! Afterall, we have been travelling through time and dealing with so much stress. It may be nice to take a bit of time to ourselves." I grin. She nods her head and gives me a smile. I roll off her and bounce to my feet, "Last one there is a rotten egg!" I squeal. I run to the door, and it opens on its own. I sprint down the hallway. *Which way??* I go left and look out of the large window overlooking a beach, I continue down, following signs until...*Ha!* I beat her. I look around the enormous room, it is built like a museum, with tons of high-tech gadgets placed around the room. I see Sylvia emerge from behind a pillar in front of me.

"*HA!* It's nice of you to join me!" She sashays towards me.

"Okay! Purr, strut yo stuff girlfriend!" I say hyping her up. She does a little spin and flips her hair. "Dayummm, baby!" I am exasperated. I skip over to her and grab her hand dragging her through the room. She twirls me around and dips me, then pulls me back up. I laugh and look around. I gesture to a glass cup. "Let's check it out."

We walk over to it, and I read the description, "This smart cup is designed to not only keep your drink cool but also keep it warm. You can adjust the settings on the bottom of the cup, and it'll do as you say. This cup does not use external heat or external cold objects."

"Okay, purr!" She says. We walk over to a faucet and fill it up with water that is steaming hot. We set the cup to cool it and instantly we watch as the water cools. I set the glass back down and continue to look. I walk over to a staircase. She reads the description this time. "Escalator-like stairs. These stairs come in a variety of materials and will transform seamlessly to match the decor of your house. These stairs are powered by themselves and don't use external power sources! The stairs also can travel multiple ways, depending on which way the user is looking." I stand on the steps, and I drift upward. I turn around and look down at Sylvia and I move down to her. I gasp.

"That's pretty cool!"

She grabs my hand and pulls me out of the room and into the game room. "VR Escape Room!" she exclaims. She runs over to it, and I follow, laughing at her. We walk into the designated area and instantly we're transformed into the room.

"Welcome! You have been locked in your bedroom and need to escape! Find the best path and don't forget about the dangers ahead!" I look at Sylvia.

"You look so realistic! Wow!" I reach out and touch her. "You feel real too!"

"Sweetie, you are touching me." She raises an eyebrow.

"Well, I am sure you don't mind. Now let's see." Around the room we see a twin-sized bed, and two nightstands on either side. On the back wall, left of the bed, is a small rectangular window. In front of this is a TV with a dresser underneath it. To the right of the bed is a small walk-in closet. The room is lit by a single light bulb in the center of the ceiling. I walk around the room, trying to find something that could be a clue. Sylvia looks in the nightstands as I walk into the closet. It appears to be a regular closet, with hangers, shelves, and clothing. I bunch the clothing up in my arms and I set it on the bed.

I look through the clothes, seeing if I can find a note or something. *Nothing.* I look at the floor, *a trapdoor somewhere maybe?* I stomp on the ground, *maybe it'll make a distinct sound?*

"Baby, come here." I look over to see the TV on the ground.

"How did you..." I shake my head and I look in the cylindrical dirt tunnel. "NOPE!" I say.

She rolls her eyes. "What's the worst that could happen?"

"UHM?? We die."

"It's fake." I squint my eyes at her.

"After you." She climbs on top of the dresser and crawls through the claustrophobia-inducing tunnel. She kicks a vent out of the wall, and we drop through, into a kitchen. On the floor is a body with a piece of paper on it, and bloody footsteps leading into another room. I pick up the note and read aloud, "Beware, she lurks! She detects movement." I shake my head quickly, "No, no, no."

"Come on scaredy-cat!" She follows the footsteps, and I do the same. She crunches down and surveys the room. She looks at me and puts her index finger to her lips. I nod, stiffly. I peek over her shoulder to see an old lady walking around the room. A knife clenched in her hands, blood dripping from the tip. I clutch Sylvia's shirt. She turns around and gives me a soft kiss on my cheek.

I spot the entrance door and assume we leave the room through there. I follow the old lady's pattern. "We go to the door?"

She shakes her head and gestures to an open vent. I watch as the lady leaves the room. We both silently dart to the opposite end of the room and into the vent. The vent leads us into a barnlike structure, we're on top of it in a loft. I spot a ladder and I point to it. She nods. I look down, and as I squint, I see a dog. "Not another dog," I whimper, quietly. She looks where I am looking and then grabs my hand and squeezes it reassuringly. We crouch over to the ladder, overlooking a massive barn door and to the left a human-sized door.

I look around and find a small tool. I grab it and throw it on the ground, opposite the door. The dog immediately runs over to it, giving me a small amount of time to climb down and exit. I climb down the ladder and swiftly crouch to the door. I grab the doorknob and fling the door open. I look for something else to throw to distract it for Sylvia. The dog begins to turn around so Sylvia yells something. The dog runs over to the back of the building, trying to find Sylvia. She crawls down the ladder and runs to me. The dog bolts towards us, but I close the door just in time.

I let out a built-up sigh and lean against the door. She pulls me into a hug. My arms simultaneously wrap around her body, mimicking her naturally.

"Congratulations! You have almost completed the escape room. Exit the fields to beat it," a voice echoes. I look at her and she kisses me.

"Let's do this!" She grabs my hand, and we sprint into the cornfields. Our feet, trampling over rows and rows of corn stocks. I hear voices and noises all around us, but I just keep running with her until we're bursting out of the field and climbing over a fence. I look behind us to see at least twenty people running after us. I grimace as my hand gets caught on a broken part of the wooden fence, penetrating my hand.

"Sylvia!" I yell. She turns to me and looks behind me.

"Oh, God. Baby!" She begins to panic, not knowing what to do. I begin to pull my hand out of the broken post, crying out in pain. "You're so strong, baby. You did so good, come on!" I jump off the fence and continue to walk, feet pounding on the freshly mowed grass. Someone comes out from behind one of the trees and pounces on Sylvia. I grip their shirt and pull them from her, my hand bleeding on their shirt, giving me an idea. I throw them on the ground and beat them unconscious. I strip their shirt from them and rip it up, using it as a bandage. "God, you're so smart!" she groans.

I smile and I tug her forward. Suddenly everything goes white. "Congratulations, you have beaten the simulation! Your injuries sustained are fictional and won't appear on your body. Play again for another randomized adventure."

We step out of the area, and I look at her smiling. "Mm, you were so sexy when you pulled that guy off of me and absolutely destroyed him."

I smirk and drape my arms over her shoulders. "It was either that or watching you get hurt. It was a no-brainer."

She giggles and kisses my lips. She looks at the digital clock on the wall. 31:30 the clock reads. "It's getting late," she murmurs as she guides me against the wall.

"Yeah?" I whisper as I pull her closer.

She nods. She rubs her lips against my cheek, her hands drifting up and down my sides.

"That hasn't stopped us before."

She smiles. "A ride in the car?"

I nod, and squeal. I think for a moment. "Actually, how about we go to our room to eat?"

She smiles at me. "That's okay! We don't have to go in the car ride yet today. We could go tomorrow."

I think for a moment weighing the two options. "Okay! Do you think they have a PC?"

She smirks. "I am sure they do, honey." I reach for her hand and lead her back to our room. "What did you wanna play?"

"You're gonna laugh," I say, a blush forming on my cheeks.

"Try me!"

"Crafters, you know what that is?"

"Of course, I do. What's wrong with that?" We walk into our room, and she heads to the area in front of the bed, where a small kitchen sits inside the open floor plan room.

I shrug. "Some might find it sad, or weird."

She turns to me and leans against the cupboards. "Well, I find it endearing. I think it's good to not let your childish side go! There's nothing wrong with being childish at times or enjoying childish things."

I look down and smile before returning my gaze. "I'm gonna go ask for a PC. You know what I just realized? We don't have any ingredients to cook with."

"Please select the dish you're looking to cook." Sylvia turns around and looks around.

"Where?" she asks.

"The book in front of you. I am an interactive cookbook. I send signals to our local food factory that someone is looking to cook something, and the ingredients are almost instantly imported into the Smart Fridge."

"Can you make anything?" she questions, intrigued.

"Yes, we're not limited to local produce."

She turns to me. "What are you fancying?"

"Porkchops with loaded baked potato and sauteed asparagus!"

"Importing ingredients, please stand by. This will take five minutes."

"Go ahead, baby. You don't have to wait. I'll be here." I nod and exit the room and walk into the reception area.

"Hello, how can I assist you?" Lumi asks me when I come into view.

"I was wondering if I could have a PC and Monitor in my room to game."

"Of course! It'll be shipped and installed in your room in ten to fifteen minutes! You can wait in your room for the time being."

"Do I have to unlock it or something so they can see it?"

She smiles. "No, we have special access to rooms. We'll need your permission to enter though."

I nod. "Okay, Thank you." I walk back to my room and find Sylvia, lying on the bed waiting for the dinner ingredients to arrive. When she catches a glance at me, she crawls to the side of the bed facing the door.

"So?"

I giggle and walk over to her. "She said they can do it. They're going to install it in our room." I smile ear to ear and sway back and forth happily. "They'll be here in ten to fifteen minutes."

"Awe, you're so cute," she murmurs. She kneels above me, still on the bed. She twirls loose strands of hair around her finger and uses her other hand to pull me closer. She wraps her arms around me and embraces me. I close my eyes and hold her back.

"Ingredients have been delivered," the cookbook interrupts. I pull away from her, but I don't get far when she squeezes my jaw with her thumb and index finger.

"It's ready," I whisper softly. She nods at me and leans in, resting her forehead against mine.

"I know." I look into her pretty brown eyes before she sighs and moves away from me and off the bed. I replace her body with mine, filling the spot on the bed she left.

"You're pretty," I say to her as she grabs the ingredients from the fridge. She looks at me briefly and smiles.

"So are you." She begins to prep the meat, seasoning it and chopping off the stems of the asparagus. I get off the bed and lean against the wall.

"Why didn't you kiss me?" I inquire, crossing my arms.

"Why didn't you kiss me?" She says back, throwing the question back at me.

I roll my eyes and bite my lower lip. "I was waiting for you."

"Likewise." She looks me up and down, a sly grin on her face.

"Come here," I say to her, gently.

"Is that a suggestion or a command?" she says with uncertainty, but she knows.

"I guess that's up to you to decide." She stops what she's doing and turns to me, crossing her arms.

"Oh, really?" she asks, tilting her head to the side.

"I didn't stutter," I tease. She squints her eyes at me and walks over to me. She pushes my back against the wall, and I smirk.

"Don't look at me like that," she purrs in my ear, her right hand caressing the side of my neck.

"Mm, I don't think I know what you're talking about. Enlighten me." She moves to look at my eyes, so soft, so pretty. It's like looking into the stars as you get lost trying to count them.

"Like that...so...I don't even know." Her voice is soft, almost muffled.

"Sylvia, kiss me," I plead as I lean into her.

"What's the *magic word?*" She traces the outline of my lips with her nail.

"Please."

"Please what?"

"Please, kiss me."

"Good," she leans in further, her soft lips brushing up against mine before they interlock. I let out a deep sigh, and my hands grip her sides, pulling her closer. Her hands land on my cheeks as she presses several elongated kisses against my lips. When she pulls away from the kiss, I whimper and tug on her shirt. She smiles as she leans back in and kisses me more. I can feel her smile on my lips, it causes the same for me. *Contagious.*

"Thank you," I murmur against her lips. She bites down on my lower lip and looks at me, lust entrancing her gaze.

"You're welcome." Before she backs away, I steal a final kiss from her.

I hear a knock on the door. She moves away from me and resumes preparing the food. I allow the computer installers access, a few robots fill the room, and install the equipment near the entrance. As quickly as they entered, they were gone just as fast. I look at the gaming setup. They gave me headphones too! I clap my hands together happily.

I sit in the chair and the monitor turns on, "Greetings! What are you wanting to play?"

I scrunch my brows. "Crafters."

"Download in progress."

I squeal and wiggle in my seat. "I want mods."

The screen launches Crafters and prompts me to log in, so I use my own log in, and it works, somehow. Something Future Crafters did was link modifications to their own launch screen. *Interesting. This is probably a supercomputer; I want to see how many mods it can take!* I begin the installation and go through tons and tons of mods, one of my favorite things about the game is installing mods.

"How's it going, honey?" Sylvia asks me from the kitchen, the smell of her cooking wafting around the room.

"Good, I am just installing mods."

She walks over to me to check out what I am doing, "You have 700."

I giggle. "It's a supercomputer, no?"

She shrugs. "I am not sure, Hun. I am no computerist."

"Hm." I look at her and hold in a laugh. "I am not sure that's a thing, *honey*."

She gasps. "That's *my* word for you! Are you mocking me?"

I open my mouth and look around. "What? I would never!" I say it sarcastically.

"Mm, I see how it is." She walks back to the kitchen and then turns back to me, blowing me a kiss. I pretend to search for it in the air and then grab it and put it on my lips. She rolls her eyes and grins.

I launch the game to see how it is. It starts up with ease. I pat the screen. "Good job! I might have to take you home with me!" I look around, playfully, and put my finger to my lips, saying 'shh' silently.

A little while later, Sylvia calls to me. "It's ready!" I pause my game and get up.

"You always cook the bestest foods!"

"The bestest?" she teases.

I nod. "Yep!"

"Thank you, sweetie. What do you wanna do tomorrow?"

I sigh and speak after I swallow. "We'll probably have to talk to that one lady; I forgot her name."

"Lumira?"

"Yeah, her." I roll my eyes and quote Erin "'This is not a vacation.'" And then I mutter under my breath, "Stupid."

I take bites out of my food as I look upward. Pondering about something.

"Penny for your thoughts?" Sylvia smiles, interrupting my thoughts.

I tilt my head to the side, thinking about where to begin. "I am trying to figure out how *this*." I gesture around us. "Works."

"Elaborate," she says as she stands up, putting our dishes aside. We walk to bed.

"How people cannot work, not need to make money, have everything shipped to them, have only one person in charge and it all seems to work." She starts to strip her shirt and jeans off and slips under the covers, I copy her. She begins to turn the light off, but I stop her. "I wanna see your face."

She gets closer to me and begins, "*Most* jobs here aren't necessary because of automation. I assume some people *choose* to work, such as Lumi. I doubt they need a person there. I think it is a mix of all three main government systems: Socialism, Communism, and Capitalism. Let me explain it one at a time. Keep in mind, I am not the creator of their system so take what I say with a grain of salt, okay?" I nod and can't help but lick my lips. *She's gonna go full hotty on me right now. I love smarty pants.* "Okay, first, Socialism. Socialism's goal is to focus on the people's needs, yes? That's essentially what they're doing. The economy isn't important, really, but they want to meet basic needs, I.E., food, transportation, housing, and health care."

She continues. "Food is shipped to your house, there's no currency so you don't have to *buy* a car, housing is free as well. Lumi even said so, 'Every single person is assigned their very own hotel room, equipped with two king-sized beds, a bathroom, and a kitchen, for however long they're on the planet.' Remember when she said that? They are making sure people aren't homeless and health care is free because again, there is no currency."

"In a perfect world, it sounds great."

She smiles at me and runs her hand up and down my arm. "Exactly, but what can Socialism lead to? Corruption, lack of people working hard, lower quality products, limited consumer choices, bureaucracy, lack of innovation, shortages or a surplus of items, limited individual freedoms, dependency on government, and some people using their power for political influence."

"Next, Communism. Some say Communism piggybacks off Socialism. Communism is where everything is controlled by the community, classless and stateless. All means of production are controlled by the community, with no private ownership, or accumulation of wealth. I think that this society is closely related to communism because *money is essentially eliminated*. You get instant access to goods and services without needing to *buy them*. Their goal is to make sure *everyone* gets the *goods and services* they need without *money*. Equality, if you will. I haven't been here long, but I don't think they divide their land into states like we do which ties into Communism. That means this *entire planet* would be the *Community*."

I laugh and state, "That sounds just as good! Everyone is equal, not money."

She shakes her head at my silly antics. "You're too goofy. The cons. The Government gaining all control, Lack of incentive, scarcity of goods, and inequality within certain parties. *Ironic, isn't it?* Authoritarianism and Repression, lack of consumer choice, economic inefficiency, brain dead society, stagnation, and limited personal freedom."

"Back up, if everything is controlled by *the community*, how does the government gain all the control?" I widen my eyes and raise my eyebrows.

"In theory it wouldn't, but in practice many involve planning *from the Government* to distribute everything. This, we already talked about, leads to its own issues. This system can also lead to bureaucratic systems, which means the big decisions are made by one person, which can lead to under or over-production, and inequality. Lack of accountability, some may make decisions to favor a certain group rather than everyone. This may be done in secret and a lot of other reasons."

I sigh. "And finally?"

"Capitalism. The *biggest thing to note about capitalism* is the aspect of *wealth*. Capitalism works *because of wealth.* This is the biggest supply and demand Government, along with competition. Individuals, corporations, and businesses own their *own goods.* This benefits entrepreneurs. The money you earn is the money you make, in the best world. Sometimes there is favoritism whether that's race, abilities, gender, sexual orientation, and other miscellaneous categories. This can all lead to, you guessed it, inequality. *Again, the irony!* How this relates to the Astrans is because the Astrans don't care if people make their own businesses, it would be a hobby though. Like Lumi."

She continues. "Maybe this would lead to *humans* being unhappy, but just because one society does this and doesn't like it, doesn't mean all won't. Without working and making money, you *can* focus on hobbies, doing things for yourself while, potentially, making others happy. Humans revolve around 'I get this, and you get that' but it doesn't *have* to be like that. You don't always need something in return for something else, you know?"

I bite my lip thoughtfully. "I understand. So, they take parts of socialism, communism, and capitalism and mush them together. It's mostly communism and less capitalism, but it is essentially a mix because you *can* own your own business, you don't rely on money, or things in return, and you have a say in your government on *all topics*, big or small and everything is distributed based on the individual's needs." I nod my head, soaking in the information she dumped on me. "This takes away the power and money aspect which, we covered, often leads to corruption."

"Yes! Lumira, maybe does control everything like a dictator, but she *doesn't* only say what *she wants*. She has everyone vote and whatever the majority agrees on is what goes and if, for some reason, something happens, she can be eliminated from power. That would be less incentivized to become a dictator because the people have a say regardless of what she says. Plus, if what they agreed on doesn't work out, they can change it."

"But also, humans like to argue, make drama. We thrive on it!"

"Let me repeat what you said, 'but also *humans* like to argue.' Keyword, baby, *humans*. As I said, not all societies are like humans. Just because humans are greedy, corrupt, and drama-hungry, doesn't mean all are. They have shown they aren't."

"What if they get bored or something, you know? It's essentially paradise where you get everything you want. Have you seen *The Good Place?* It didn't work out."

"It's not paradise because bad things can happen, just because the majority is great, doesn't mean there's not a small percentage that isn't. Plus, look at why we're here. The Vorakons. That isn't perfect! There's *always* something to do to better society. Nothing is perfect."

"Besides you." I grin and poke her cheek.

She giggles and kisses my cheek. "I couldn't have said it better myself."

I frown as I look at her, my eyes fall between us, and I sigh.

"Did I say something wrong...or?" She plays with my hair.

"No...I just. Don't want this to end." I look back up at her, and I swallow.

"Why does it have to end? You'll have me as long as you want," she whispers. She leans into me and places a soft kiss on my lips, her hand moving to rest on my cheek. I push her hand harder against my cheek, my eyes closed as the kiss fades.

"We're eventually going to have to go back to present Earth and leave this bed. Leave each other's arms. I don't want to." I squeeze her hand and pull her into a hug. My body does not want to let go. *What if it's the last time I'll get to hold her this close?*

"Honey..." Her voice is shaky, only making me squeeze her harder. She sits up a little and lays some of her weight on me. Her skin so soft against mine, her arms just as desperately wrapped around me.

"Sylvia," I murmur softly against the crook of her neck.

"Yes?" she murmurs back.

"Would you, one day, want to marry me?" I've thought about it often.

She pulls away and smiles at me. "Yes." Such a simple reply, but the way she is looking at me, tells me she truly means it. The way her eyes are sparkling, the corners of her lips raised as far as they can go. The little creases near her eyes smiling at me. "Would you?" she questions. *Would this be considered getting engaged if I say yes?*

"Without a doubt in my mind, yes." *The absolute emotional mess, from curious, to happy, sad, confused.*

She leans down and places kisses on my lips, a smile imprinted on her features. "We should get to bed, baby girl."

I nod and sigh. "Okay."

Chapter Nine: An Unforgiving Meeting

"**A**re you ready, Hun?" Sylvia asks as I look around the room. "Ready as I'll ever be! Hint: I don't wanna go!" I throw in a playful smile.

"Let's try to make the best out of it. Maybe Lumira isn't a bitch anymore and the Vorakons have surrendered!" *Such a glass half-full gal.*

I roll my eyes. "Yeah, right. Besides only half of those options are possible."

"And which one is that?" She walks over to me. *She looks so darling.* We went to get some new clothes earlier today and she got this cute flower dress, it is white with roses on it. She said, "*I wanted to look nice for you.*"

I smirk. "The Vorakons surrendering. Plus, we don't even know if they're bad. They're so dramatic, they haven't even attacked yet."

"*Yet.* That doesn't mean they won't. Now come on, baby, we must go!" She grabs my hand and pulls me out of the door. I groan as we walk out of the hostelry.

"See ya!" Lumi calls to us. I turn my head and wave at her.

"You can let go of me, now," I say to Sylvia.

"You *want* me to let go of your hand?"

I sigh and roll my eyes. *Sas.* "No."

"That's what I thought."

"'That's what I thought,'" I mock under my breath.

She stands to the side of the car and turns to me. She leans in and whispers in my ear. "You better lose the attitude, missy. It won't look good when we're trying to get on Lumira's good side."

I cross my arms at her and pout. She gives me the death glare and I groan throwing my head back. "Whatever!"

"That wasn't convincing. Try again."

I take a deep breath. "Fine, I won't be mean to Lumira." I basically have to choke the words out.

"Good girl. Now get into the car." Celestia opens the doors and allows us access. I step in and Sylvia gets in through the other door.

"Greetings! Where to?" Celestia asks.

"We need to go to SISA." *Sylvia, Sylvia, Sylvia. Why she gotta be such a bully. It's not fair. Why do I have to be nice to Lumira?*

"Well, life isn't fair." She pats my leg and smiles. *Did I say what I said out loud?* "No, I am just a mind reader."

"Stop that!" I glare at her, and she laughs. A smile on her face.

"You're so cute when you're cranky."

"Would you like to start a discussion topic?" Celestia asks.

"Sure!" I think for a moment. "I got nothing."

I look at Sylvia and she shrugs. "How about...we just relax, eh?"

I squint my eyes and pucker my lips, thoughtfully. "Or..." I begin.

She tilts her head to the side, looking me up and down. "Or?"

I get closer to her, my hand on the right side of her neck. I bite her earlobe. "Or we could talk about whether or not having a purpose in life gives you meaning."

She sighs. *What's wrong? Didn't think that's what I'd say?* "Okay, I think not."

"Oh? Explain."

"Well, just because you do or don't have a 'purpose' that doesn't mean your life has more or less meaning."

"Precisely. If you live your life to the fullest, you complete your purpose. You don't have to exist to achieve *something,* but people feel better when you do," Celestia chimes in.

"Do you remember when we talked about *your* purpose? I said, 'Have you ever thought that this is your purpose?' Referring to us saving humanity?"

She nods. "Yes, and I didn't understand what you meant."

"Exactly, and I said 'What we're doing right now. You met me, I wanted to save the world, you came with me, and we are doing it together. I think this is why we're here. Why you're here, to help people, and yourself. You have a purpose, but that doesn't mean it will fall into your hands. Sometimes you must dig a little deeper to figure it out.' I still believe we all have a purpose. Even if it's something simple. Something unexpected. Having a purpose *does* give you meaning but if you didn't find it, your life wouldn't be meaningless."

She chews on her bottom lip. "I suppose...but you can't forget about the last part of that conversation."

I crinkle my eyebrows. "What's that?"

"I had asked you 'Maybe you're part of my purpose.' I disagree with that now...you *are* my purpose."

"Awe, baby." I smile at her and giggle. *So sappy but I love it.*

"I mean it. I definitely would not be where I am right now without you."

"You mean on another planet about to be face-to-face with a raging bi-"

Celestia cuts me off. "Speaking of, we're here!"

"And no, I meant with you, happy, content, and safe."

And the sap keeps coming. I pout. "You're too sweet."

We step out of the car, and she starts walking up the steps, but I stop her. "Wait!" I say quickly. I begin patting my pockets and she puts her hands on her hips.

"Girl, what are you up to, now?" She questions, raising a brow. I pull two pairs of sunglasses out of my pocket, and I hand one to her. I slip it on. "Wow."

"Now, we're baddies. Let's get it." I flip my hair and walk to the building, pretending I am walking in slow motion. She looks at me shaking her head and smiling.

"Ridiculous."

"You love it." We walk into the building and are instantly greeted by Erin.

"And the main characters arrive!" Erin says.

"That's right." I pose. I lean into Sylvia, and I whisper, "I told you."

"Too silly," she whispers back, smiling.

"What's the tea? The drama? The dilemma. Hit us," I say as we walk into the meeting room.

"The issue is nothing. Nobody has lifted a finger. The Vorakons haven't moved, and we haven't tried to contact them again," Erin proceeds. "We are hoping you guys have an idea."

"Us? Are you sure Lumira doesn't have a good idea? I recall her being pretty smart," I say sarcastically. Sylvia hits my leg, making me jump. "I mean, wow, I am so flattered."

"Oh, save it! Yeah, I shouldn't have said what I said yesterday, you had every right to punch back, and *okay* maybe I was a *little* jealous of you two. But *whatever.*"

I chuckle. "Why jealous?"

She sighs and grinds the back of her molars. *This is gonna be good!* "Because you all are like...so happy and it's just gross. Like, barf. But also, I admire it, but also barf, you know?"

I look at Sylvia and she raises her eyebrows at me and rubs her lips together. I silently plead to say what's on my mind, and she gives in, obviously. I am hot. "Oh, so you're just lonely?"

Lumira tilts her head to the side and cringes. "Yeah, yeah I suppose."

"And that's why you're so bitter."

"Yes..."

"And that's why everyone hates you?"

Sylvia glares at me. *Too far?* Apparently not because Lumira nods. "Yes..." Instantly I feel bad for her. I stand up and wrap my arms around her in an awkward hug.

"There, there, Lumira, you have what? Five million more years left. You'll be okay. You'll find someone," I say trying to comfort her.

"You really think so?" she questions.

I look at Sylvia and she nods quickly. "Of course, I do! You're hot...um...smart. Really smart. Chicks dig that."

"You think so?" she asks.

I look at Sylvia and she smirks and mouths, "You started it."

I look at Lumira and I give her my best, "Of course!" I can muster. "But you have to change your ways, you know."

She nods. "Of course." I sit back down, and Sylvia grabs my hand from under the table. I look at her and she gives me a 'you did good' nod. *Score!*

"So...now we must talk about what to do. Reluctantly, I am considering going up to them..." Lumira begins.

I look at Sylvia and I raise my eyebrows. She rubs her thumb on my hand, so I don't lash out. *Such soft skin.*

"And how would that go down? What if it is just a dead end?" Erin interrogates.

She shrugs. "I have no idea...what else are we going to do? It's either that or fight them, and that would be *really* starting a war."

"We can take a vote. With your people," I suggest.

"Excellent idea! We don't have to be alone in this!" I beam and look at Sylvia.

"Good job, baby," she mouths to me.

"I am sending out a pull. Three options: wait it out, go and try to communicate with them directly, or attack them. The voting usually only takes a few minutes."

"We could also vote with each other to know where we all are?" Vaelor suggests. *She speaks once again!* Since she is the first Astran on this planet, I am surprised she doesn't speak more.

"Okay! Everyone heads down, no peeking," Lumira says. Everyone in favor of fighting raise a hand." After a few seconds, she says, "Lower hands. All in favor of talking to them directly, raise a hand." I raise my hand this time. "Alright, lower your hands. Finally, all in favor of waiting it out." After a few seconds, "Okay, you can look. So, no one wanted to attack, one person wanted to wait, and everyone else was in favor of talking directly with them!" *Hm. I wonder who the odd one out is? Seraphina? Erin?...Sylvia?*

I look at people's expressions to figure out who it is. *Definitely Seraphina.* Her tendrils are blue, and all the other Astran's tendrils are green. I love that tendril stuff. Although Seraphina the guide seemed so kind, I didn't think she'd be one to attack.

"I have an unrelated question!" I say.

"What is it, Natalie?" Lumira asks, genuinely.

"Why do you all have tendrils? Did you make them? And how do your feet and hands work? Did you make those too?" I question.

"Good question. We were born with the tendrils, but we used biological sciences to have our bodies adapt to certain terrains and our hands are just normal, I guess. For us."

I look at Sylvia and I whisper in her ear. "I am on a roll with good questions, aren't I?"

She smiles. "Mm, maybe I'll have to reward you on our downtime."

I look into her eyes, my body fighting the urge to kiss her. "Again, with the PDA! What is up with you two?" Benjamin says, annoyed.

"No, seriously," everyone agrees.

I shrug. "When y'all find love, you'll do the same thing." Everyone groans. *Now I am obligated to kiss her.* I grab her head to look at me and I kiss her, unashamed. She raises her eyebrows in surprise and gasps against my lips but kisses me back. When I back away I peck her lips again. I turn to everyone, and I cross my arms. "Got somethin' to say? Say it!"

Everyone stays quiet. *I know, we're hot. It's okay to admit. #powercouple.*

I look back at her and she mouths, "One more, please." *How sweet.* I smile and lean back in, kissing her again. I run my hands through her hair before we're stopped by a clearing of a throat. I keep my eyes on her, pouting. She fixates her attention off me and looks around.

"The votes are in! Can I get a drumroll?" Lumira says. Erin drums his tentacles against the table. "Looks like we're going to go up there and try to negotiate with them. Any volunteers?"

I look around the room. Wondering who's gonna do it. Suddenly I hear a voice that makes my stomach drop. "I'll do it," Sylvia says.

Chapter Ten: Uncharted Perils: A New Journey Ends

"Please!" I call out to Sylvia as she walks towards the spaceship. I grab her hand, stopping her. "Baby," I whimper, tears streaming relentlessly down my cheeks. "Please."

She takes a shaky breath as I watch all her walls crumble before me. "Honey..." She whispers. She looks toward her copilot. "Could you give us a second?" She nods and walks away. She takes a few steps toward me, her hand on my cheek. I look down but she tilts my head up and wipes the tears off my cheek.

"You can't do this...what if...something bad happens to you...I can't lose you...I feel like I just got you." I grip the sides of the space suit, and new streams of water roll down my cheeks.

She leans into me, our lips interlocking. My grip on her tightens. "I am not going to leave you here. If something happens, I promise I will do all I can in my power to get out."

"But what if it's not enough? What if..." I gasp at the thought; her ship being shot and her body lifeless in space. I put my hand over my mouth, my eyes too blurred to see her. *What if this is the last time I'll be able to kiss her lips? The last time I'll touch her skin? The last time I'll look into her beautiful brown eyes? The last time.*

"It will be baby. I will come back to you, I promise." She swipes my hair out of my face.

"But you can't promise that!" I cry out. Anger is starting to build. I run my hands through my hair, and I turn around. *Don't let your back be the last thing she sees of you.* I turn back to face her.

"This was your idea, honey...I know you didn't count on me going...but would you really feel this way if someone else went up there?"

"It's..." I look into her eyes. I step closer. "Different...you're different. *I love you.*"

Even though we've dated for over a year, neither of us has said those three words. I have been saving it. "Baby..." She grabs my hand and kisses it. "*I love you too.*" She backs away and blows me a kiss. I grab it, and put it to my lips, not even cracking a smile, as I watch her step into the spacecraft. In a blink of an eye, I feel like it's all gone. All of the memories of her, the touch of her skin on mine, the sound of her laugh, her smile, her freckles, her silky-smooth hair, and her raspy voice when she is feeling *spicey*. I think about the first time we met. The way her face looked when she saw me, the concern in her voice as she called to me. *I loved her the first time I met her.* Now, she's gone. Slipped between my fingers. *Gone.*

S ylvia's Solo Journey

I step onto the ship, and I look out the window to see Natalie on the ground, her head tucked into her knees. Her body shakes as she sobs. I broke her poor heart. *I did that. I made her feel that way. Why am I doing this again?* "Are you coming?" the copilot asks.

"Yeah..." I choke on the syllables, a lump in my throat reforming. "Yes," I say firmer. I take a deep breath, and I tear my eyes off her disheveled and broken body in a heap on the ground. *Why am I doing this?* I slip my helmet on, remembering the time she took it off of me. The way her eyes danced around my face as if she was mapping my features out to save it as a keepsake, so she never forgets anything. I close my eyes as I encapsulate myself in the moment. Her words lingered in my mind, 'We can take off our spacesuits' she had said. I wish we had. I shake my head and walk to the cockpit. This spaceship is small, enough to fit two people only.

The Co-piolet gives me a rundown of the levers, buttons, and switches. I nod my head, trying to remember it all. "This button is only for emergencies! It will eject you!" *Got it. Button on left, don't press unless there's an emergency.* "This craft is one of the best we have. It is equipped with state-of-the-art technology. This craft eclipses their technology. If something happens, if we go onto their ship...if *you* go onto their ship, this ship is our only chance to get away. The craft starts up and rises instantly off the ground, like a hovercraft. I grip my holographic energy-based gun in my hands. *If they take it, they can't use it. It's tailored to me.* "Ready?"

I nod stiffly. "Sure," I manage to squeak out. The craft bursts forward at instant light speed. Memories flood my mind repeatedly. Her hands on me when as we watched the Aurora together. *She looked so good that night.* Her whole body was lit by the ascension of the moonlight. The Aurora colors painted her on the hood of the car. Her lips pressed on mine as Synthia played us that romantic song, the lyrics dance in my mind 'In your arms, I've found my place. With every beat, our love will soar.' I pick out in my mind. I look down at myself. *If I found my place, why am I doing this?*

"We're coming close to their ship. I'd get ready for any...technical difficulties." I look up, to see a massive Alien-like ship coming quickly into view. She slows our craft down and positions the door to enter their ship. Both open. I grab my gun as I look at her. "Give me a call if you need help."

I nod. I get out of my seat, and I pull myself onto their ship, gravity kicking in once I enter. *How did they make gravity?* "Human," A gritty voice says. I look around, biting my lip. *What the fuck?* "Drop your firearms." I close my eyes before setting my gun down on the floor and stepping away from it. *I don't know how many Vorakons there are in front of me, but there might be a lot.*

"Who are you?" I ask, looking around the white, empty ship. I can hardly see a thing, it's so bright.

The person chuckles. "Oh, darling." *Don't fucking call me that.* "We're part of you. We're your mind, your soul, your life."

"Cut the bullshit. Who the hell are you? Show yourself, now!" *So angry. Anger. Hate. Boil inside of me, I can't control it anymore...I hate that I left her for this bullshit.*

"No need for anger. We're here to help."

"Help what...exactly?" I ask. *Calm yourself, calm yourself. Take your own advice.*

"You believe the Astrans are good beings? If that's true, explain this." A noise echoes inside the craft.

"Those stupid humans and Stellarborns are so gullible. Ahhaha, how could we hack into their ships. I can't believe they fell for it. There was never an 'intergalactic catastrophe' it was only ever one ship. I just wanted an excuse to see those pathetic humans, Sylvia and Natalie, for myself. Nobody can make a perfect world. That's why we devour the ones that try to be. I have gone soft, but not for long," a muffled voice says under their breath.

"Who is that? How did you get that? What's happening?" My heart races in my chest. *Natalie. I left her there. I left her there. Alone.*

"It's all a lie, my friend. Your Astran friends. They're Gods. They devour every civilization they find until there's nothing left."

"How do you know this?" A figure forms in front of me. *An Astran?*

"I started it."

"What about Vaelor?" I question instantly.

"Indeed, the first female to transform, not the first on Astrana. Also, I am male. The last male of my species. The real reason for that was Lumira and Vaelor, attacked us. They used their power against us, and everyone just sat there and did nothing, due to fear. They slaughtered my race in a bloodbath of hate." He floats closer to me. "Lumira and I were in love. We dated for centuries, got married, and had kids. Three little girls. I had fallen out of love with Lumira, and she turned to Vaelor for guidance. They were close since Lumira was the second to transform. I only had two options at the time, and I connected to Lumira more. When more people began to form, I fell out of love with Lumira. She couldn't handle it and turned her back on me." *That's why she was bitter about our relationship...she was jealous.* "She couldn't kill me. Instead, she banished me. She grew evil. She hated herself and took it out on everyone else. They both were kicked off the planet and migrated to other planets, some including Viper, Emrys, and Dubeunus, Asking for help. A species called Arboreans took her and Vaelor in."

He continues. "They befriended each planet and slowly took over those worlds. Stripping them of everything they have."

"What about the other people there? Lumi?" Lumi was nice, she gave us advice.

"AI. The only real Astrans are Vaelor and Lumira living on each planet they settled on. They took everything from everyone on each place, including their technology and started building their own 'species.' She has lost herself and I fear she's going to take you two down with her. She doesn't care about the others...the Stellarborns or humans. You folks called her out, and it opened new scars and wounds for her. Initially, she cared about my ship, but not for long. Once she saw you two, a happy couple. Everything flooded back to her."

"My...baby..." I murmur under my breath. I press my fingers to my lips, trying to remember her lips on mine from before I left.

"I understand your concern, and I will help you. I need to fix some of my own mistakes too."

"How do you know all this if you were banned?" I question.

"I met a civilization, they're like Starlight Sylphs. Their species name is Zephyrites. They helped me. Gave me insight into their own technologies. This ship, for example, is like an invisible cloak. I can see out, but others can't see me or the ship. Something must've gone wrong with the cloaking system and the cloaking ability broke, revealing my identity."

"How can you know about everything that's going on down there?"

"*I* hacked into *her* system centuries ago. I always have watched and followed her very closely."

"Why? I thought you were over her?"

"Closure. We haven't talked since the day we broke up. She wouldn't hear a word that I was saying …I guess there wasn't much to say but clearly, closure needs to happen. We must go back down there so we can both save our girls." He begins to float around the ship before we enter the cockpit. The ship creaks as we begin to move. It jolts to the left, swiveling back to her planet.

"What about weapons? Do you know what's happening down there?" I say hastily.

"Lumira is dragging Natalie under the SISA. Into a cellar. This cellar gradually heats up until the person passes out from heat exhaustion and dies. She likes to torture her victims with a slow burn when it's personal to her. The only way to get into Natalie's cell is Lumira's hand." I begin hyperventilating. *No, no, no. This must be a dream. I must be dreaming. This isn't happening. We're home, we're safe.* Tears begin to fill my eyes. *I left her, I left her, I left her. She pleaded with me to stay. She pleaded. I left anyway!* "Don't blame yourself. You wouldn't have known."

"I am going to marry her," I say sternly. "When we get back to Earth, I am going to marry her. I love her, I am in love with her. I never want anyone else but her wrapped in my arms for all eternity."

"Then let's get down there! We hopefully won't need a gun but if we do, take this. It's designed to kill AI and Astrans. We have thick skin so it's hard to penetrate it. Also, your other friends, Erin, President Montgomery, and Benjamin, have fled. Everyone that you came with has left the planet. Lumira threatened their lives if they didn't." He lands the ship, and we both get out quickly. The gun connects to my hand, wrapping around my arm. This allows me to disguise it. *Cool.* We both run to the doors. Me first. He stays outside.

"Well, well, well, the second little piggy makes it out alive."

"Shut up, Lumira! I know everything! You had love and it slipped from your fingertips! That isn't our fault! Stop cursing everyone because one guy didn't want you."

"HE USED ME! He told me I was enough! *I was enough when he had nobody else to choose from.*"

"Please, just give me Natalie. Please, Lumira. *I love her...*if you remember what it's like losing someone you love...you'd give her back to me." Tears begin to ricochet onto the floor. Lumira stares at me, her tendrils turning a rainbow of colors.

"How did you even learn about all of this..." She puts her hand over her mouth.

"I told her." The guy, whom I still don't know the name of, comes into view. Stepping into the building.

Her features drop. Her body relaxes. *She still loves him.* "Arius...?" He walks over to her.

"I am sorry about what I did, Lumira...it was wrong, but I didn't use you...I did love you. I fell in love with you, Lumira...It doesn't mean that because I fell out of love, I never loved you to begin with." He wipes tears off her face. "I remember how amazing you were when we fell in love...you were happy. You loved everyone...your tendrils never turned any other color but green. This...isn't who you are."

She looks down. "I know. But I can't go back...all the other males are dead...because of me."

"I'm not. I am willing to start over...if you are."

"But I thought you didn't want me anymore..."

"Right person, wrong time...we rushed it. I needed time. Now I am here. Asking for a second chance."

"Arius...I can't. I just can't. I have changed since then. I am not the person you knew. Maybe I never was the person you loved," Lumira says to him.

"Lumira. You can change. You can always change. I am sorry for what I did. I am sorry for how I treated you but think of the kids...Aria, Nova, and Selene. They are still alive. Trying to find their place in this world. The Astrans need you back...your kids need you back." He pauses his speech and continues to look deep into her eyes. "I need you back."

"I..." she looks at me. "I want you back...I have all this time...I was just...scared to move on and even if I tried, I couldn't. I never thought men were stupid and only wanted women, I just thought *you* were stupid for leaving me."

He smiles at her, his tendrils a bright green. "Does that mean you want to try this again?" he asks her softly. She nods.

"Yes, Arius. I am. But if you mess up again...I don't think I can pick up your pieces again," she whispers.

He leans in and kisses her. "I understand. But...for us to work I have one condition?"

"Anything," she murmurs.

"Let Natalie go."

She nods. "Come on Sylvia." I rush over to her. My heart beats swiftly in my chest. *Please be okay, baby. Hang on.* She opens a camouflaged door, and we walk down some steps. The corridor is made from stone which makes it look even more eerie and dungeon-like.

"Natalie!" I call out as she comes into view. The high temperature fades as Lumira unlocks the door. "Baby, baby. Say something!" I scoop her up in my arms. My hands frantically brush strands of hair out of her face. I begin to stand and carry her upstairs. When I set her down and look at her body, my tears drip onto her cheek. "Please," I whimper as I rest my hand on her cheek and my forehead against hers. "Please," I plead again. I begin replaying events from us in my head as I hold her body close to mine.

"Are you okay?" I ask frantically as I kneel next to her body.

"I don't think so," her voice echoes and cracks as she tries to speak. When she tries to move, I frantically stop her.

"Don't move! Do you live close by?"

"Do you need anything?" I ask her. She stares at me. Her jaw falls ajar as she scans my features.

"Um," she says. She looks so flabbergasted. "Yes, no. No, I am good." She pauses. "Well, I am a little thirsty."

*"**K**iss me." I plead with her. She did. My whole world stopped once her lips touched mine. The way she touched my skin was as if I was fragile and she didn't want to break me. Her eyes were so soft and blue as they looked at me before we kissed.*

"It's beautiful," *she said in awe. She turned to look at me, a perfect opportunity to kiss her. I hovered above her and leaned down, kissing her little face all over before pressing my lips against hers. My body lit on fire as I relived our first kiss and every kiss after that. It was so emotional I cried. Then Synthia played the song, and it was so perfect.*

Natalie's Point of View

Tears spill onto my cheeks, making my body jolt in surprise. I feel a hand pressed on my cheek and a forehead against mine. "Please," She whispers several times.

"Sylvia," I say almost inaudible. She backs up and looks at me, her face flushed with fear, tears filling her pretty caramel eyes.

"Oh my God!" Her body folds around me, my legs wrap around her body as she sobs into my arms. "I thought I lost you! I thought..." she trails off.

"I am here." I squeeze her tighter, bits and pieces of what happened uncoiling in my mind. "I love you, I love you," I repeat, loving how the words feel, finally finding their way out of my lips. They'll never go back into hiding.

"I love you too! I love you more than anything in this world. I am sorry I left you! I am so, so, so sorry!" she sobs as she presses her lips against mine. I slowly sit up, her body following mine.

"Baby, you didn't know. It's not your fault," I whisper before kissing her more, her hands in my sweaty hair, and my body swimming into her lap.

"I know. I just...seeing you so upset...it hurt."

"It's okay...you thought you were doing what was best. Your intentions were good, honey. You cared for my well-being. That's all I see. You and me."

References

NCADV. n.d. "National Statistics." National Coalition Against Domestic Violence. Accessed August 17, 2023. https://ncadv.org/statistics.

Epilogue

After what feels like *years* of flying, driving, and time traveling, we finally step back into our present time and into our home. I let out a long sigh of relief as I flop down onto the couch. "Oh my God." I groan. I sit up to find Sylvia looking at me. "What?" I squint my eyes at her.

"Nothing, I am just going to take a shower." She smirks and sashays into the bathroom. I watch her, curiously. I get up and follow her.

"What are you up to?" I question.

She smiles and looks me up and down. "I told you; I am going to shower." She closes the door and begins to whistle as she undresses. *This girl.* I shake my head and sit back down on the couch. I look around, happy to finally be able to relax, knowing it's all over.

After a while, the shower turns off, and the door opens, a towel wrapped around her body and a towel on her head. I tilt my head to the side as a cloud of steam emerges from behind her. *Is it hot in here or is it just her?* I open my mouth to say something to her, but she disappears into the bedroom. "Go shower, baby girl!" She calls out to me. I do as she says, going into the shower after her.

"What are you planning?" I question as we leave the house. Her choice of attire is nothing short of tantalizing—a form-fitting dress that sumptuously accentuates every curve, a dark shade of crimson that seems to mirror her presence. The dress flows flirtatiously just passed her thigh, revealing just enough to pique my imagination.

Her delicate shoulders are adorned with gracile straps, leaving her collarbone exposed, deliberately. Her neckline plunged modestly, teasing glimpses of her skin, while maintaining the flavor of mystery. Her waist is synched, accentuating her hourglass figure. I let my eyes trace every curve that she possesses.

Golden hoop earrings adorn her earlobes, shimmering in the evanescent lighting.

"Mmm," she hums. "I guess you'll just have to wait and see, little thing." We climb into Synthia, Erin let us take her back to the past. It's disguised as a regular sedan. She whispers something under her breath to Synthia, adding to the confusion. The car starts, electricity coursing through its veins as it starts speeding off to the mysterious location. To my surprise, it transforms stealthily into plane mode. Erin upgraded Synthia so that it turns into planes like ones here. It advances with technology as we advance so the government can't detect it is from the future. Since it travels so fast, it can't be detected by any governmental places. Erin and even Lumira seemed adamant that it was undetectable so I will take their word for that.

"You will reach your destination in 10 minutes. We will be traveling under light speed for this trip at 7,800 miles (about 12.5 thousand km) per hour. Thank you for flying with JetBula X." I look at her so confused.

"Baby, I don't understand..." I feel so underdressed. I threw on a pair of jeans and a silk V-neck t-shirt. She leans toward me and puts her fingers against my lips.

"Shhh," She whispers. My eyes dart all over her body as I nod. "Look at me," her tone is suggestive, making my heart beat rapidly in my chest, a blush seeping towards my cheeks. My eyes fly back to hers, as I whine looking at her. *What is she planning?* I lean closer to her, trying to steal a kiss, but she backs away. I proceed to lean in farther, but she keeps backing away. I whine again, sticking out my bottom lip, and pouting.

"Sylvia" I whimper as I try to touch her, but she grabs my hands and puts them behind my back.

She smiles as she rubs her lips against mine. "Patience is a virtue." She bites my bottom lip and maintains eye contact as she looks at me.

"Please seat yourselves securely in your seats, we will be descending briefly," I whine, not wanting to leave the closeness, but she gently pushes me back in my seat.

"Stay," She commands in my ear. I take a deep breath as she backs away, trying to not let her take all the breath out of my lungs. *Breathtaking, figuratively and metaphorically.* I keep my eyes on her as she ruffles her curly hair. *When did you curl her hair? What is happening?* I continuously fight the urge to lean over and kiss her inviting lips.

"Now, descending. You will reach your destination shortly." *Destination too....? WFSA? Oh, God. Please don't be another mission.* We land, Synthia doesn't turn back into a car so we can get back home swiftly...when whatever this is, is over...We step out of the plane and Sylvia guides me to the overlook of Washington D.C.

"What are-" she cuts me off, with a simple touch of my cheek.

"Baby," she whispers as she looks at me, leaning closer to me.

"Yes?" I whisper back, my heart *pound, pound, pounding* in my chest.

"Every second I am with you, I feel like I can be myself. I feel whole. You complete my life, and I could never have asked for anyone better...When I left you and saw the look on your face, it broke my heart. Your body on the ground, sobbing *for me.* I felt...empty, and when I saw you laying in the cell, it felt like a part of me left with you. A part only you can provide. I want to spend the rest of my life with you. I want to *be* with *you.*" I put my hand over my mouth, tears spilling out of my eyes. *Is she...*she proceeds to get down on one knee, looking up at me.

Tears stream down her cheeks as she pulls out a white box. She opens it and inside yields a beautifully crafted gold ring. "Baby..." I whisper my eyes wide as I look at her. My body trembles as she looks up at me.

"Natalie, will you marry me?" she asks, through shaky breaths. *She took me here to relive our first kiss...*

I nod quickly. "Yes! Absolutely I will marry you!" I say eagerly. She rises, grabs the ring, and slips it on to my finger. I throw myself at her, my arms wrapping around her, our bodies interlocking as we cry together. I jump up on her, as I kiss her eagerly. Tears mix in with the mint of her toothpaste and the aroma of her flowery perfume. She carries me to the plane; the doors are already open. She sits me down in the passenger seat and sits on my lap. I pause as I look at her. "When..." I stutter, clearing my throat. "When did you get it?"

She presses her body against mine, looming over me. "Do you remember when we were coming home and there was a MarketHub we passed?" I nod. "I said I had to get something inside, and I did but only to disguise what I was really doing. I went to the jewelry store next door. I already knew your ring size, and what you like so it was a no-brainer. I knew I wanted to marry you when I was on the big ship, Arius's ship. I confessed it to him out loud and it felt good to finally say those words."

I return my hand to my mouth as I strain my neck to look up at her, new tears welling up in my eyes. My hand leaves my mouth and drifts to her cheek, my thumb pulling her bottom lip down, my own lips part as I look at her. "You're absolutely dazzling." After I say that she leans down and kisses me aggressively. My arms wrap around her as I pull her into me.

"So are you." She groans in between passionate kisses.

"Mm," I whimper. "I am so underdressed." She grips my cheeks with her thumb and index finger.

"You're never underdressed in my eyes." She smirks and leans down, whispering in my ear. "Even when you aren't dressed."

Afterword

I hope that my story offered you more than just something enjoyable to read. Specifically, I wanted to shed some light on the critical issues of domestic violence and the impact of social media on our society.

Every year, there are hundreds of thousands of reported cases of domestic abuse in the United States alone. Sadly, many individuals fail to recognize the warning signs of an abusive relationship, including friends and family. If you read the content in this book and identify any red flags in your relationships, I encourage you to reach out to someone you trust. You deserve to be treated with respect and kindness. It doesn't have to be an intimate relationship either. Any type of relationship can become abusive.

Additionally, if you found yourself disagreeing with my perspective on social media, I understand. I invite you to take a moment to reflect on my words. Social media has the power to damage relationships and erode self-esteem. Businesses exploit these platforms to engage people, especially young adults, and drive profits relentlessly.

This is a societal concern that warrants attention. As we move forward, it's crucial for us to address the implications of social media and find ways to use these platforms in healthier and more constructive ways. I believe social media is one of the *best* and *worst* things that has come into our lives.

Thank you for joining me on this journey. Your engagement with these topics means a great deal to me. Let's continue the conversation and work towards positive change.

If you did enjoy this story, it would be amazing if you gave me a review on Amazon! Reviews help authors so much!

Sincerely,

Amelia Lucas

Acknowlegment

I would like to acknowledge the people who have not only helped me write and/or publish my book, but who have just supported me through my writing journey.

First, I would like to thank my mom for publishing this piece of work. If not for you, this book would not be out there for people to read.

Thank you, Penny, for editing this book with me and very coming on this journey with me. You have not only helped me edit this book, but you have also worked *with me* in making my story come to life. Thank you.

To my friends, Caleigh and Karla. You two have been with me through thick and thin and I am so grateful to have you gals in my life. I don't know what I would do without you.

To the person who created my cover, Annette Marie, thank you for working so diligently in creating my cover! You were so thoughtful, understanding, and efficient in what you have created for me. Thank you!

Finally, I'd like to thank Mrs. Mitchell. You are not only my art teacher but also one of my most favorite teachers and friends. You not only supported my books in reading them, but you have also helped me with my covers, and hyping me up when I need it most! Thank you so much for all you do for me and your students.

1

9 798224 126279